From One Generation to Another

Henry Seton Merriman

1st WORLD
LIBRARY
Literary Society

From One Generation to Another

Henry Seton Merriman

© 1st World Library – Literary Society, 2004
PO Box 2211
Fairfield, IA 52556
www.1stworldlibrary.org
First Edition

LCCN: 2004195308

Softcover ISBN: 1-4218-0139-6
Hardcover ISBN: 1-4218-0039-X
eBook ISBN: 1-4218-0239-2

Purchase *"From One Generation to Another*
as a traditional bound book at:
www.1stWorldLibrary.org/purchase.asp?ISBN=1-4218-0139-6

1st World Library Literary Society is a nonprofit
organization dedicated to promoting literacy by:

- Creating a free internet library accessible from any
  computer worldwide.
- Hosting writing competitions and offering book
  publishing scholarships.

From One Generation to Another
contributed by Tim, Ed & Rodney
in support of
1st World Library Literary Society

CONTENTS

I. THE SEED.. 7

II. SUBURBAN.. 15

III. MERCURY 24

IV. FREIGHTED... 34

V. AFTER NINETEEN YEARS.. 43

VI. FOR HIS COUNTRY 53

VII. ON THE ROOF OF THE WORLD............................... 64

VIII. RELIEVED.. 73

IX. RE-CAST 82

X. A LAST THROW... 92

XI. A CARPET KNIGHT 99

XII. BAD NEWS.. 108

XIII. ON THIN ICE 118

XIV. THE CURSE OF A GOOD INTENTION................... 128

XV. THE TOUCH OF NATURE.. 137

XVI. THE SPIDER AND THE FLY.................................... 147

XVII. TWO MOTIVES.. 157

XVIII. LIKE SHIPS UPON THE SEA 167

XIX. AT HURLINGHAM 178

XX. IN A SIDE PATH 187

XXI. ALONE 197

XXII. ACROSS THE YEARS 206

XXIII. AND THE TIME PASSES SOMEHOW 216

XXIV. A STAB IN THE DARK 226

XXV. FROM THE JAWS OF DEATH 235

XXVI. BALANCING ACCOUNTS 245

XXVII. AT BAY 255

XXVIII. THE LAST LINK 264

XXIX. SETTLED 273

CHAPTER I

THE SEED

Il faut se garder des premiers mouvements, parce qu'ils sont presque toujours honnétes.

"Dearest Anna, - I see from the newspaper before me of March 13, that I am reported dead. Before attempting to investigate the origin of this mistake, I hasten to write to you, knowing, dearest, what a shock this must have been to you. It is true that I was in the Makar Akool affair, and was slightly wounded - a mere scratch in the arm - but nothing more. I have not written to you for some months past because I have been turning something over in my mind. Anna, dearest, there is no chance of my being in a position to marry for some years yet, and I feel it incumbent upon me ..."

This letter, half written, lay on a camp table before a keen-faced young officer. He ceased writing suddenly, and, leaping to his feet, walked to the door of his bungalow, which was open to the four winds of heaven. In doing this he passed from the range of the lazy punkah flapping somnolently over table and bed. It may have been this sudden change to hotter air that caused him to raise his hand to his forehead, which was high and strangely rounded.

"By George!" he said, "suppose I do it that way!"

He walked rapidly backwards and forwards with the lithe actions of a man of steel, a light weight, of medium height, keen and quick as a monkey. His black eyes flitted from one object to another with such restlessness that it was impossible to say whether he comprehended what he saw or merely looked at things from force of habit.

He was dark of hair with a sallow complexion and a long drooping nose - the nose of Semitic ancestors. A small mouth, and the chin running almost to a point. A face full of interest, devoid of distinct vice - heartless. Here was a man with a future before him - a man whose vices were all negative, whose virtues depended entirely upon expediency. Here was a man who could be almost anything he liked; as some men can. If expediency prompted he could be a very depôt of virtues; for his body, with all the warmer failings of that part of humanity, was in perfect control. On the other hand, there was no love of good for goodness' sake - no conscience behind the subtle eyes. All this, and more, was written in the face of Seymour Michael, whose handwriting had dried some moments before on the half-filled sheet of letter-paper.

He returned and stood at the table with slightly bowed legs - not the result of much riding, although he wore top-boots and breeches as if of daily habit - but a racial defect handed down like the nasal brand from remote progenitors. He looked at letter and newspaper as they lay side by side - not with the doubtfulness of warfare between conscience and temptation, but with a calculating thoughtfulness. He was not wondering what was best to do, but what the most expedient.

Those were troublesome times in India, for the Mutiny was not quelled, and each mail took home a list of killed, slowly compiled from news that dribbled in from outlying stations, forts, and towns. Those were days when men's lives were made or lost in the Eastern Empire, for it seems to be in Fortune's balance that great danger weighs against great gain. No large wealth has ever been acquired without proportionate risk of life or happiness. To the tame and timorous city clerk comes small remuneration and a nameless grave, while to more adventurous spirits larger stakes bring vaster rewards. The clerk, pure and simple, has, within these later years, found his way to India, sitting side by side with the Baboo, and consequently it is as easy to make a fortune in London as in Calcutta and Madras. The clerk has carried his sordid civilisation and his love of personal safety with him, sapping at the glorious uncertainty from which the earlier pioneers of a hardier commerce wrested quick-founded fortunes.

Seymour Michael had come into all this with the red coat of a soldier and the keen, ambitious heart of a Jew, at the very nick of time. He saw at once the enormous possibilities hidden in the near future for a man who took this country at its proper value, handling what he secured with coolness and foresight. He know that he only possessed one thing to risk, namely, his life; and true to his racial instinct, he valued this very highly, looking for an extortionate usury on his stake.

At this moment he was like Aladdin in the cave of jewels: he did not know which way to turn, which treasure to seize first.

Anna - dearest Anna - to whom this half-completed letter was addressed, was a person for whom he had not the slightest affection. At the outset of his career he had paused, decided in haste, and had resolved to make use of the passing opportunity. Anna Hethbridge had therefore been annexed *en passant*. In person she was youthful and rather handsome - her fortune was extremely handsome. So Seymour Michael went out to India engaged to be married to this girl who was unfortunate enough to love him.

In India two things happened. Firstly, Seymour Michael met a second young lady with a fortune twice as large as that of Miss Anna Hethbridge. Secondly, the Mutiny broke out, and India lay before the ambitious young officer a very land of Ophir. He promptly decided to cut the first string of his bow. Anna Hethbridge was now useless - nay, more, she was a burthen. Hence the letter which lay half-written on the table of his bungalow.

He paused before this wrong to a blameless woman, and contemplated the perpetration of a greater. He weighed pro and con - carefully withholding from the balance the casting weight of Right against Wrong. Then he took up the letter and slowly tore it to small pieces. He had decided to leave the report of his death uncontradicted. It was morally certain that five weeks before that day Anna Hethbridge had read the news in the printed column lying before him. He resolved to leave her in ignorance of its falseness. Seymour Michael was not, however, a selfish man. All that he did at this time, and later in life - all the lives that he ruined - the hearts he broke - the men he sacrificed were not offered upon the altar of Self (though the distinction may appear subtle), but sold to his career. Career was this man's god. He wanted to be great, and rich, and powerful; and yet he was conscious of having no definite use for greatness, or riches, or power when acquired.

Here again was the taint of the blood that ran in his veins. The curse had reached him - in addition to the long, sad nose and the bandy legs. The sense of enjoyment was never to be his. The greed of gain - gain of any sort - filled his heart, and *ennui* secretly nestling in his soul said: "Thou shalt possess, but not enjoy."

He was conscious of this voice, but did not understand it then. He only burned to possess; looking to possession to provide enjoyment. In this he was not quite alone - with him in his error are all men and women. And so we talk of Love coming after marriage - and so women marry without Love, believing that it will follow. God help them! That which comes afterwards is not even the ghost of Love, it is only Custom. This was the spirit of Seymour Michael. He had already acquired one or two objects of a vague ambition; and, possessing them, had only learnt to be accustomed to them - not to value them.

There was no elation in the thought that he was freed from the encumbrance of Anna Hethbridge by a chance misprint. Neither was there hesitation in turning accident ruthlessly to his own advantage. There was only a steady pressing forward - an unceasing, unwearying attention to his own gain.

In those days news travelled slowly, and the personal had not yet taken precedence in journalism. In the anxiety for the State, the Individual was apt to be overlooked. Seymour Michael counted on six months of oblivion at the least - he hoped for more, but with characteristic caution acted always in anticipation of the worst.

He had scarcely thrown the newspaper aside when a comrade entered the bungalow carrying another copy of the same journal.

"I say, Michael," exclaimed this man, "do you see that you're put in among the killed?"

"Yes," replied Seymour Michael, without haste, without hesitation. "I have already written to contradict it. Not that there is any one to care whether I am dead or alive. But it might do me harm in Leadenhall Street. I can't afford to be dead even for a week when so much promotion is going forward."

This was artistic. Most of us forget to preserve our own characteristics in diverging from the truth. The tangled web is only woven when *first* we practise to deceive. Later on the facility is greater, the handling superior, and the web runs smooth and straight. Seymour Michael was apparently no novice at this sort of thing. He was even at that moment making mental note of the fact that up-country mails were in a state of disorganisation, and a letter which was never written may easily be made to have miscarried later on.

But even he could not foresee everything - no one can. Not even the righteous man, much less the liar.

"Do you mean to say," pursued the newcomer, "that you are not writing to your family about it - only to the Company?"

"That is all."

"Rum chap you are, Michael," said the other, lighting a cheroot. "Heartless beggar I take it."

"Not at all. The simple fact is that I have no one to write to. I only possess one or two distant relatives, and they would probably be rather sorry than otherwise to have the report contradicted."

The younger officer - a mere boy - with a beardless, happy face, walked to the door of the bungalow.

"Of course there is always this in it," he said carelessly. "By the time the contradiction reaches home the news may be true."

Seymour Michael laughed lamely. A joke of this description made him feel rather sick, for a Jew never makes a soldier or a sailor, and they are rarely found in those positions unless great gain is holden up.

With this pleasantry the youth departed, leaving Michael to write the letter which he had advised as written. As he drew the writing materials towards him he cursed his brother officer quietly and politely for a meddling young fool. He wrote a formal letter to the Company - the old East India Company which administered an empire with ledger and daybook - calling their attention to the mistake in the newspaper, and begging them not to trouble to give the matter publicity, as he had already advised his friends.

This done, he proceeded with the ordinary routine of his daily life. Such men as this are case-hardened. They carry with them a conscience like the floor of an Augean stable, but they know how to walk thereon. Moreover, he was one of those who assign to their dealings with men quite a different code of morals to that reserved for women. His was the code of "not being found out." Men are more suspicious - they find out sooner: *ergo* the morals to be observed *vis à vis* to them are of a stricter order. Railway companies and women are by many looked upon as fair game for deception. Consciences tender in many other respects have a subtle contempt for these two exceptions. Many a so-called honest man travels gaily in a first-class carriage with a second-class ticket, and lies to a woman at each end of his journey without so much as casting a shadow upon his conscience.

Seymour Michael carried this code to the farthest limit of safety. All through the months that followed he went about his business with a clear conscience and a heart slightly relieved by the removal of Anna Hethbridge from his path to prosperity. He served his country and the Company with a keenness of foresight and a soldierly exposure of the lives of others which did not fail, in the course of time, to bring him in a harvest of honours and rewards. Neither did he put his andle under a bushel, but set it in the very highest candlestick available.

But, as has been previously stated, he could not foresee everything. He did not know, for instance, that his cheroot-smoking subaltern - a youth as guileless as he was indiscreet, for the two usually go together - possessed a memory like a dry-plate. He did not foresee that a passing conversation in an Indian bungalow might perchance photograph itself on the somewhat sparsely covered tablets of a man's mind, to be reproduced at the wrong moment with a result lying twenty-six years ahead in the womb of time.

CHAPTER II

SUBURBAN

L'amour fait tout excuser, mais il faut être bien sûr qu'il y a de l amour.

Miss Anna Hethbridge loved Seymour Michael with as great a love as her nature could compass.

When the news of his death reached her, at the profusely laden breakfast-table at Jaggery House, Clapham Common, her first feeling was one of scornful anger towards a Providence which could be so careless. Life had always been prosperous for her, in a bourgeois, solidly wealthy way, entirely suited to her turn of mind. She had always had servants at her beck and call, whom she could abuse illogically and treat with an utter inconsequence inherent in her nature. She had been the spoilt child of a ponderous, thick-skinned father and a very suburban mother, who, out of her unexpected prosperity, could deny her daughter nothing.

Three months after the receipt of the news Anna Hethbridge went down into Hertfordshire, where, in the course of a visit at Stagholme Rectory, she met and became engaged to the Squire of Stagholme, James Edward Agar.

A month later she became the second wife of the simple-minded old country gentleman. It would be hard to say what motives prompted her to this apparently heartless action. Some women are heartless - we know that. But Anna Hethbridge was too impulsive, too excitable, and too much given to pleasure to be devoid of heart. Behind her action there must have been some strange, illogical, feminine motive, for there was a deliberation in every move - one of those motives which are quite beyond the masculine comprehension. One notices that when a woman takes action in this incomprehensible way her lady friends are never surprised; they seem to have some subtle sympathy with her. It is only the men who look puzzled, as if the ground beneath their feet were unstable. Therefore there must be some influence at work, probably the same influence, under different forms, which urges women to those strange, inconsequent actions by which their lives are rendered miserable. Men have not found it out yet.

Anna Hethbridge was at this time twenty-four years of age, rather pretty, with a vivacity of manner which only seemed frivolous to the more thoughtful of her acquaintances. The idea of her marrying old Squire Agar within six months of the untimely death of her clever lover, Seymour Michael, seemed so preposterous that her hostess, good, sentimental Mrs. Glynde, never dreamt of such a possibility until, in the form of a fact, it was confided to her by Miss Hethbridge, one afternoon soon after her arrival at the rectory.

"Confound it, Maria," exclaimed the Rector testily, when the information was passed on to him later in the evening. "Why could you not have foreseen such an absurd event?"

Poor Mrs. Glynde looked distressed. She was a thin little woman, with an unsteady head, physically and morally speaking; full of kindness of heart, sentimentality, high-flown principles, and other bygone ladylike commodities. Her small, eager face, of a ruddy and weather-worn complexion - as if she had, at some early period of her existence, been left out all night in an east wind - was puckered up with a sense of her own negligence.

She tried hard, poor little woman, to take a deep and Christian interest in the welfare of her neighbours; but all the while she was conscious of failure. She knew that even at that moment, when she was sitting in her small arm-chair with clasped, guilty hands, her whole heart and soul were absorbed beyond retrieval in a small bundle of white flannel and pink humanity in a cradle upstairs.

The Rector had dropped his weekly review upon his knees and was staring at her angrily.

"I really can't tell," he continued, "what you can have been thinking about to let such a ridiculous thing come to pass. What are you thinking about now?"

"Well, dear," confessed the little woman shamedly, "I was thinking of Baby - of Dora."

"Thought so," he snapped, with a little laugh, returning to his paper with a keen interest. But he did not seem to be following the printed lines.

"I suppose she was all right when you were up just now!" he said carelessly after a moment, and without lowering his paper.

"Yes, dear," the lady replied. "She was asleep."

And this young mother of forty smiled softly to herself as if at some recollection.

This happiness had come late, as happiness must for us to value it fully, and Mrs. Glynde's somewhat old-fashioned Christianity was of that school which seeks to depreciate by hook or by crook the enjoyment of those sparse goods that the gods send us. The stone in her path at this time was an exaggerated sense of her own unworthiness - a matter which she might safely have left to another and wiser judgment.

Presently the Rector laid aside the newspaper, and rose slowly from his chair.

"Are you going upstairs, dear?" inquired his tactless spouse.

"Um - er. Yes! I am just going up to get - a pocket-handkerchief."

Mrs. Glynde said nothing; but as she knew the creak of every board in the room overhead she became aware shortly afterwards that the Rector had either diverged slightly from the path of which he was the ordained finger-post, or that he had suddenly taken to keeping his pocket-handkerchiefs in the far corner of the room where the cradle stood.

It will be readily understood that in a household ruled, as this rectory was, by a sleepy little morsel of humanity, Anna Hethbridge was in no way hindered in the furtherance of her own personal purposes - one might almost add periodical purposes, for she never held to one for long.

The Squire was very lonely. His boy Jem, aged four, would certainly be the happier for a mother's care. Above all, Miss Hethbridge seemed to want the marriage, and so it came about.

If Anna Hethbridge had been asked at that time why she wanted it, she would probably have told an untruth. She was rather given, by the way, to telling untruths. Had she, in fact, given a reason at all, she would perforce have left the straight path, because she had no reason in her mind.

The real motive was probably a love of excitement; and Miss Anna Hethbridge is not the only woman, by many thousands, who has married for that same reason.

The wedding was celebrated quietly at the Clapham parish church. A humiliating day for the stiff-necked old Squire of Stagholme; for he was introduced to many new relatives, who, if they could have bought up Stagholme and its master, were but poorly equipped with the letter "h." The bourgeois ostentation and would-be high-toned graciousness of the ladies, jarred on his nerves as harshly as did the personal appearance of their respective husbands.

Altogether it was just possible that Squire Agar began to realise the extent of his own foolishness before the effervescence had left the champagne that flowed freely to the health of bride and bride-groom.

The event was duly announced in the leading newspapers, and in the course of a few days a copy of the *Times* containing the insertion started eastward to meet Seymour Michael on his way home from India.

Anna Agar came home to Stagholme to begin her new life; for which peaceful groove of existence she was by the way totally unfitted; for she had breathed the fatal air of Clapham since her birth. This atmosphere is terribly impregnated with the microbe of bourgeoisie.

But the novelty of the great house had that all-absorbing fascination exercised over shallow minds by anything that is new. At first she maintained excitedly that there was no life like a country life - no centre more suited for such an ideal existence than Stagholme. For a time she forgot Seymour Michael; but love is eminently deceitful. It lies in a comatose silence for many years and then suddenly springs to life. Sometimes the long period of rest has strengthened it - sometimes the time has been passed in a chrysalis stage from which Love awakens to find itself changed into Hatred.

Little Jem, her stepson - sturdy, fair, silent - was her first failure.

"Come to your mother, dear," she said, with unguarded enthusiasm one afternoon when there were callers in the room.

"I cannot go to my mother," replied the youthful James, with his mouth full of cake, "because she is dead."

There was an uncompromising matter-of-factness about this simple statement, made in all good faith and honesty, which warned the second Mrs. Agar to press the matter no farther just then. But she was so intent upon exhibiting to her neighbours the maternal affection which she persuaded herself that she felt for the plain-spoken heir to Stagholme, that she took him to task afterwards. With great care and an utter lack of logic she devoted some hours to the instruction of Jem in the somewhat crooked ways of her social creed.

"And when," she added, "I tell you to come to your mother, you must come and kiss me."

This last item she further impressed upon him by the gift of an orange, and then asked him if he understood.

After scratching his head meditatively for some moments, he looked into her comely face with very steady blue eyes and said:

"I don't think so - not quite."

"Then," replied his stepmother angrily, "you are a very stupid little boy - and you must go up to the nursery at once."

This puzzled Jem still more, and he walked upstairs reflecting deeply. Years afterwards, when he was a man, the sunlight falling on the wall through the skylight over the staircase had the power of bringing back that moment to him - a moment when the world first began to open itself before him and to puzzle him.

It happened that at that precise time when Mrs. Agar was endeavouring To teach her little stepson the usages of polite society, a small, keen-faced man was standing near the table in the smoking-room in the Hotel Wagstaff at Suez. He was idly turning over the newspapers lying there in the hopes of finding something comparatively recent in date.

Presently he came upon a copy of the *Times*, with which he repaired to one of the long chairs on that verandah overlooking the desert which some of us know only too well.

After idly conning the general news he glanced at the births, deaths, and marriages, and there he read of the recent ceremony in the parish church of Clapham.

"D - n it!" he muttered, with that racial love of an expletive which makes a Jew a profane man.

In addition to a strong feeling of wounded vanity that Anna Hethbridge should so soon have forgotten him, Seymour Michael was distinctly disappointed that this heiress should no longer be within his reach. The truth was, that the young lady in India had transferred her valuable affections, with all solid appurtenances attaching thereto, to a young officer in the Navy who had been invalided at Calcutta.

To men who intend, despite all and at any cost, to get on in the world the first failures are usually very bitter. It is only those who press stolidly forward without expecting much, who profit from a check. Seymour Michael was just the man to fail by being too acute, too unscrupulous. He was usually in such a hurry to help himself that he never allowed another the very fruitful pleasure of giving.

In India his zeal had led him into one or two small mistakes to which he himself attached no importance, but they were remembered against him. He had cruelly thrown aside Anna Hethbridge when a richer marriage offered itself. Now he had missed both bone and reflection, and he sat with a smile on his dark face, looking out over the dreary desert.

CHAPTER III

MERCURY

The evil is sown, but the destruction thereof is not yet come.

James Edward Makerstone Agar was not at the age of five the material from which the heroes of children's stories are evolved. He was not a good boy, nor a clean, nor particularly interesting. He was, however, honest - and that is *déjà quelque chose*. He was as far removed from the "misunderstood" type as could be wished; and he was quite happy.

Before his stepmother had laid aside the title and glory of a bride, he had, by his deadly honesty, made her understand that even a child of five requires what she could not give him - namely, logic. Had she been clever enough to reason logically she might have undermined the little fellow's innate honesty of character, despite the fact that he lacked a child's chief incentive to learn from its mother, namely, the sympathy of heredity.

Gradually and steadily Mrs. Agar "gave him up," to make use of her own expression. She was one of those women who either fear or despise that which they do not understand. She could scarcely fear Jem, so she

Henry Seton Merriman

persuaded herself that he was stupid and unattractive. At this time there came another influence to militate against any excess of love between Jem and his stepmother. It came to her, for he was ignorant of it. And this was the knowledge that before long the little heir's undisputed reign in the nursery would come to an end.

With a suburban horror of being a long distance from the chemist, Mrs. Agar protested that she could not possibly remain at Stagholme during the ensuing winter, and that her child must be born at Clapham. It was vain to argue or reason, and at last the Squire was forced to swallow this second humiliation, which was quite beyond his wife's comprehension. He only dared to hint that all the Agars had seen the light at Stagholme since time immemorial; but feelings of this description found no answering note in her practical and essentially commonplace mind. So Mr. And Mrs. Agar emigrated to Clapham, leaving Jem behind them.

It happened that a few days after their arrival at the stately house overlooking the Common, a young officer called to see Mr. Hethbridge, who was at that time one of the Directors of the East India Company. Now it furthermore happened that this young soldier was he whom we last saw smoking a cheroot in the doorway of Seymour Michael's bungalow in India. As chance would have it, he called in the evening, and the estimable Mr. Hethbridge, warmed into an unusual hospitality by the fumes of his own port wine, pressed him to pass into the drawing-room and take a dish of tea with the ladies. The subaltern accepted, chiefly because it was the Director's self that pressed, and presently followed that short-winded gentleman into the drawing-room - thereby shaping lives yet uncreated - thereby unconsciously helping to work out a chain of events leading ultimately to an end which no man could foresee.

"Yes," he said, in reply to Mrs. Agar's question, "I am just back from India."

It happened that these two were left almost beyond earshot at the far end of the room. The old people, among whom was Mrs. Agar's husband, were settling down to a game of whist. Mrs. Agar was leaning forward with considerable interest. This was not a mere passing curiosity to hear further of a country and of an event which have not lost their glamour yet.

The very word "India" had stirred something up within her heart of the presence of which she had been unsuspicious. She was as one who, having a closed room in her life, and thinking the door thereof securely barred, suddenly finds herself within that room.

"Whereabouts in India were you?" she asked, with a sudden dryness of the lips.

"Oh - I was north of Delhi."

"North of Delhi - oh, yes."

She moistened her lips, with a strange, sidelong glance round the room, as if she were preparing to jump from a height.

"And - and I suppose you saw a great deal of the Mutiny?"

Even then - after many months, in a drawing-room in

peaceful Clapham - the young man's eyes hardened.

"Yes, I saw a good deal," he answered.

Mrs. Agar leant back in her chair, drawing her handkerchief through her fingers with jerky, unnatural movements.

"And did you lose many friends?" she asked.

"Yes," answered the young fellow, "in one way and another."

"How? What do you mean?" She had a way of leaning forward and listening when spoken to, which passed very well for sympathy.

"Well, a time like the Mutiny brings out all that is in a man, you know. And some men had less in them than one might have thought, while others - quiet-going fellows - seemed to wake up."

"Yes," she said; "I see."

"One or two," he continued, "betrayed themselves. They showed that there was that in them which no one had suspected. I lost one friend that way."

"How?"

It was marvellous how the merest details of India interested this woman, who, like most of us, did not know herself. Moreover, she never learnt to do so thoroughly, thereby being spared the horrid pain of knowing oneself too late.

"I made a mistake," he explained. "I thought he was a gentleman and a brave man. I found that he was a coward and a cad."

Something urged her to go on with her pointless questions - the same inevitable Fate which, according to the Italians, "stands at the end of everything," and which had prompted Mr. Hethbridge to bring this stranger into the drawing-room.

"But how did you find it out?"

"Oh, I did not do it all at once. I first began by a mere trifle. It happened that this man was reported dead in the Gazette - I showed it to him myself."

The young officer, who was not accustomed to ladies' society, and felt rather nervous at his own loquacious-ness, kept his eyes fixed on his boots, and did not notice the deathly pallor of Mrs. Agar's face, nor the convulsive clutch of her fingers on the velvet arm of the chair.

She turned right round, with a peculiar movement of the throat as if swallowing something, and made sure that the whist-players were interested in their game. In that position she heard the next words.

"He did not even take the trouble to write home to his friends. I thought it rather strange at the time, and told him so. Later on I heard the truth of it. I heard him tell some one else that he was engaged to a girl in England, and he thought it a very good way of getting out of the engagement."

"You heard him tell that, with your own ears?"

"Yes; and he seemed to think it a good joke."

Mrs. Agar was shuffling about in the chair as if in pain.

Then she asked again in a strangely metallic voice, "Did he say that he - did not love her?"

"Yes, the cad!"

"He cannot have been a nice man," she said, with that evenness of enunciation which betrays that the tongue is speaking without the direct aid of the mind.

The young officer rose with a glance towards the clock.

"No," he said, "he was not. He did other things afterwards which made it quite impossible for a man with any self-respect whatever to look upon him as a friend."

"Did he," asked Mrs. Agar, "say anything about her personal appearance? Was it that?"

The subaltern looked puzzled. It was as well for Mrs. Agar that he was not a man of deep experience. Instead of being puzzled he might suddenly have seen clear.

"No - no," he replied. "It was not that. It was merely a matter of expediency, I believe."

But, womanlike, Mrs. Agar did not believe him. She sat while he made his farewell speech over the whist-table, but as he went to the door she rose and followed him slowly.

In the hall she watched the servant help him on with his coat - her features twisted into a stereotype smile of polite leave-taking.

"By the way," she said, with a sickening little laugh, "what was the man's name - your friend, whom you lost?"

"Michael - Seymour Michael."

"Ah! Good-night - good-night."

Then she turned and walked slowly upstairs.

We are apt to read indifferently of human ills, whether of the flesh or the soul. We are apt to overlook the fact that what we read may apply to us. Some of us even bear upon us the mark of hereditary disease and refuse to believe in it. Then suddenly comes a day when a pain makes itself felt - a dumb, little creeping pain, which may mean nothing. We sit down and, so to speak, feel ourselves. Before long all doubt goes. We have it. The world darkens, and behold we are in the ranks of those upon whom we looked a little while back with a semi-indifferent pity.

It was thus with Mrs. Agar. As some play with nature, so had she played with her own heart. She had heard of a consuming love which is near akin to hatred. She had read of passion which is stronger than the strongest worldliness. She had smilingly doubted the existence of the broken heart pure and simple. And now she sat in her own room, numbly, blindly feeling herself, like one to whom the first warning of an internal deadly disease has been manifested. She was conscious of something within herself which she could not get at, over which she had no control.

With quivering lips she sat and wondered what she could do to hurt this man. She did not only want to inflict bodily pain, but that other gnawing pain of the heart which she herself was now feeling for the first time. And through it all there ran the one thought that he must die. It was strange that hate should first teach her that love is a living, undeniable reality in the lives of all of us. She had never realised this before. Her bringing-up, her surroundings, all her teaching had been that money and a great house, and servants, and carriages were the good things of this life, the things to be sought after.

She had been conscious of a vague admiration for Seymour Michael, and that was the full extent of her knowledge of herself. This admiration took the worldly form of a conviction that he was destined one day to be a great man, and she had a strongly developed, common-minded desire to be a great lady.

There are some things in this life which to a moderate intelligence are quite unmistakable. Most of us, having left childhood behind, recognise at once an earthquake, and death. Love is as unmistakable when it really comes. And Anna Agar, having suddenly learnt to hate Seymour Michael, knew that she had loved him with that one all-absorbing love which comes but once to a woman.

She was not a deep-thinking or a subtle woman. Her actions were usually based upon impulse, and her one all-absorbing desire now was to see him, to speak to him face to face. In this indefinite longing there was probably a vulgar love of vituperation - the taint of her low-born ancestors.

She wanted to shout and shriek her hatred into the evil face of the man who had tricked her. She wanted to frighten him, to threaten, to lash him with her tongue. For she was conscious all the while of her own inability to harm him. Without defining the thought, her common-sense taught her one lamentable, unjust fact; namely, that unless a woman is loved by the object of her wrath she can hardly make him suffer.

She rose at last, and, lighting the candles on the writing-table, she proceeded to write to Seymour Michael. Even in this epistle the natural cunning of her nature appeared.

"DEAR SEYMOUR " - she wrote on a sheet of paper bearing the address of the house in which she was staying, the roof under which Seymour Michael had first paid his careless tribute to her wealth - "I learnt by accident this evening that your regiment has returned to England. If you are in London, I hope you will make time to come and see me. Come to-morrow evening at four, if that time is convenient to you. ANNA."

She purposely signed her Christian name only, purposely refrained from vouchsafing any personal news. She did not know how much or how little he might know.

Ringing for her maid, she sent the letter to the post, addressed to Seymour Michael, at the Service Club, of which she knew him to be a member. Then she went to bed to toss and turn all night. The doctors, good, portly Clapham practitioners, had warned her in the usual way to spare herself all bodily fatigue and mental worry for the sake of the little one. It is so easy to urge each other to spare all mental worry, and so eminently useful.

CHAPTER IV

FREIGHTED

I shall remember while the light lives yet,
And in the darkness I shall not forget.

Seymour Michael was no coward where hard words
and no hard knocks were to be exchanged. His faith in
his own keenness of intellect and unscrupulousness of
tongue was unbounded.

He smiled when he read Anna Agar's letter over a
dainty breakfast at his club the next morning. The
cunning of it was obvious to his cunning comprehension, and the fact of her suppressing her newly-
acquired surname only convinced him that she knew
but little about himself.

That same evening at four o'clock he presented himself
at the lordly hall-door of Mr. Hethbridge. Since first he
had raised his hand to this knocker, fingering his letter
of introduction to the East India director, Seymour
Michael had learnt many things, but the knowledge
was not yet his that indiscriminate untruths are apt to
fly home to roost.

Anna Agar had easily managed to send her mother out
of the house; her husband spent his days as far from

Clapham as circumstances would allow. She was seated on a sofa at the far end of the room when Seymour Michael was shown in, and the first thing that struck her was his diminutiveness. After the hearty country gentlemen who habitually carried mud into the Stagholme drawing-room, this small-limbed dapper soldier of fortune looked almost puny. But there is a depth in every woman's heart which is only to be reached by one man. Whatever betide them both, that one is different from the rest all through life.

Neither of these two persons spoke until the servant had closed the door. Then, as is usual in such cases, the more indifferent spoke first.

"Why did you never write to me?" said Seymour Michael, fixing his mournful glance on her face.

"Because I thought you were dead."

"You never got my letter contradicting the report?"

"No," she answered, with so cheap a cunning that it deceived him.

"And," he went on, with the heartlessness of a small man, for large men respect woman with a deeper chivalry than every puny knight yet compassed, "and you did not trouble to inquire. You did not even give me six months' grace to cool in my grave."

"How did you send your letter?" she asked, with a suppressed excitement which he misread entirely.

"By the usual route. I wrote off at once."

"Liar! liar! liar!" she shrieked.

She had risen, and stood pointing an accusatory finger at him. Then suddenly the dramatic force of the situation seemed to fail, and she burst out laughing. For some seconds it seemed as if her laughter was getting beyond her control, but at last she checked it with a gurgle.

The complete success of the trap which she had laid for him almost disappointed her. Few things are more disappointing than complete success. She hated him, and yet for the sake of the one gleam of good love that had flickered once in her essentially sordid heart, she had nourished a vague hope that he would clear himself - that at all events he would have the cleverness to see through her stratagem.

"Liar!" she repeated. "In this room last night - not twenty-four hours ago - Mr. Wynderton told me all about it. He said that you told several men in his presence that you did not love me, and that your death reported in the papers was the best way of breaking off the engagement."

Seymour Michael's eyes never wavered. For once they were still, with that solemn depth of gaze which tells of the curse laid on a smitten, miserable race. It was strange that before honest men and women his glance wavered ever - he could never meet honest eyes; but looking at Anna Agar they were as steady as those of a true man.

"Wynderton," ho said, "the man whose promotion I stopped, by a report against him for looting."

When Nature makes a fool in the guise of a woman she turns out a finished work. Mrs. Agar's eyes actually lighted up. Seymour Michael saw; but he knew that he had no case. Nevertheless, in view of the Squire's advanced age (a fact of which he had made sure), he attempted to carry through a forlorn hope.

"And you believe this man before you believe me?" said Michael. It is strange how often one hears the word "believe" on the lips of those whose veracity is doubtful.

Now it happened that Mr. Hethbridge had spoken of Wynderton at breakfast that morning in terms which left no doubt as to the untruth of the statement just made in regard to him. But even this would have been passed over by the woman who had a natural tendency towards falsehood herself, had not Seymour Michael made a hideous mistake. A wiser man than any of us has said that there is a time for all things. Most distinctly defined is the time for making love. More men come to grief by making too much love than too little. Seymour Michael, being heartless, deemed erroneously that this was a propitious moment to essay the power which had once been his over this woman.

He accompanied his reproachful speech with a tender glance, which in olden times had never failed to call forth an answering look of love in her eyes. Now, it suddenly aroused her to realise the extent of her hatred. In some subtle way it humiliated her; for she looked back into the past, and saw herself therein a dupe to this man.

"No!" she cried, and her raised voice had a sudden twang in it - suggestive of the streets; of the People.

"No - you needn't trouble to make soft eyes at me. I know you now - I know that what that man said was true. He called you a coward and a cad. You are worse! You are a Jew - a mean, lying Jew."

There are few greater trials to a man's dignity than vituperation from the lips of a woman. She walked towards him, clumsily, menacingly and raised her hand as if to strike him.

Seymour Michael's brown face turned yellow beneath her blazing anger.

"Sit down!" he commanded, "and don't make a fool of yourself."

He was mean enough to pay her back in her own coin - the paltry, loud-ringing coin which is all that a woman has.

"I do not mean to wrangle," he said coolly; "but I may as well tell you now that I never cared a jot for you. I was laughing at you in my sleeve all the time. I did not want you but your money. I concluded that the money would be too dear at the price, so I determined to throw you over. The way I chose to do it was as good as any other, because it saved me the trouble of writing to you."

Anna Agar had obeyed him. She was sitting down in a stiff-backed arm-chair, looking stupidly at the pattern of the carpet as if it were something new to her. Between physical pain and mental excitement she was beginning to wander. She was the sort of woman to lose control over her mind with a temperature of one hundred and one.

Michael looked keenly at her. He had a racial terror of physical ailment. He saw that something was wrong, but his knowledge went no further. He had never seen a woman faint, so limited had been his experience of the sex.

"Come," he said consolingly, "it is all for the best. We made a mistake. In a few years we shall look back to this, and thank Heaven for saving us many years of unhappiness. We are not suited to each other, Anna. We never should have been happy."

It was characteristic of the man to be more afraid of a fainting fit than of a broken heart.

He went to her side and stood, not daring to touch her, for fear of arousing another of those fits of passion in her which neither of them seemed to understand. At length she spoke in a singular monotonous tone which an experienced doctor would have recognised at once as the speech of a tongue unguided for the time being. She did not look up, but kept her eyes fixed on the carpet as if reading there.

"Some day," she said, "I will pay you back. Some day - some day. I do not know how, but I feel that you will be sorry you ever did this."

Twenty-five years afterwards these words came back to him in a flash. They passed through his brain - conglomerate - in a flash, in a hundredth part of the time required to speak them.

Even at the time of hearing them, spoken in that voice which did not seem to belong to Anna Hethbridge at all, he turned pale. For all the hatred that burnt within her like a fire smouldered in the deliberate tones of her voice. Hatred and love can teach us more in a moment than the experience of a lifetime; for through either of them we see ourselves face to face. This hatred made Anna Agar in twenty-four hours, and the woman thus created went through a lifetime unchanged.

Michael went towards the bell.

"I am going to ring," he said, "for your maid."

"Twice," she muttered in the same vague way.

He obeyed her, ringing twice.

Presently the woman came.

"Your mistress," said Michael in a low voice to her at the door, "has been suddenly seized with faintness. I leave her to you."

Without looking round he passed through the doorway and out into his own self-seeking life. But Anna Agar's revenge began from that moment. To a man of his nature, in whose veins ran the taint of a semi-super-stitious Oriental blood, there was a nameless terror in the hatred of a human being, however helpless. Surely the hell of the coward will be a twilight land of vague shadowy dangers ever approaching and receding.

In such a land Seymour Michael moved for some months, until he returned to India; and there, in the daily round of a new life, he gradually learnt to shake off the past. The world is very large despite chance meetings. It is easy enough to find room for two even in the same county, with the exercise of a little care.

Twenty-five years elapsed before these two met again, and then they only had time to exchange a glance. By that time the result of their own actions had passed beyond their control.

Seymour Michael walked across the Common, which was in those days still wild and almost beautiful; and on the whole he was pleased with the result of this interview. He knew that it was destined to come sooner or later - he had known that all along; and it might have been worse. It is characteristic of an untruthful nature to be impervious to the shame of mere detection. In Eastern countries the liar detected smiles in one's face. Detection is to an Oriental no punishment; something more tangible is required to pierce his mental epidermis.

Being quite incapable of a strong love this man was innocent of consuming hatred. He therefore vaguely wondered whether the day might come wherein he would once more lay siege to the affections of Anna Agar, a rich widow.

Had he seen the face of the woman whom he had just left as it lay at that moment, hardly less pale than the pillow between the fluted mahogany pillars of a huge four-post bed, he would not have understood its meaning. He would never have divined that the dull gleam shining between her half-closed eyelids was simple hatred of himself, that the restless, twitching lips were whispering curses upon his head, that the half-stunned brain was struggling back to circulation and thought for the sole purpose of devising hurt to him.

Seymour Michael, ignorant of all this, went peaceably

back to his club, where he dressed, dined, and proceeded to pass the evening at a theatre.

That night, while he was displaying his diamond studs in the stalls of Drury Lane Theatre, was born into the world - long before his time - a child, Arthur Agar, destined to walk the smoothest paths of life, literally in silk attire; for he grew up to love such things.

But the ways of Nature are strange. She is very quiet; patient as death itself. She holds her hand for years - sometimes for a generation - but she strikes at last.

She is more cruel than man, or even than woman which is saying much, She is the best friend we have, and the worst foe, for she never forgives an outrage.

Nature raised her hand over this puny, whimpering child, Arthur Agar. She never forgot a mother's selfish passion. She forgets nothing. When first he opened his little pink lids upon the world he looked round with a scared wonder in a pair of colourless blue-grey eyes; and that vague look of expectation never left his eyes in later life. It almost seemed as if the infant orbs could see ahead into the future - could discern the lowering hand of outraged Nature.

This hand was suspended over the ill-fated, poorly-endowed head for years, then Nature struck - hard.

CHAPTER V

AFTER NINETEEN YEARS

A sharp judgment shall be to them that be in high places.

"Yes, dear. I have great news for you to take back to your mother. Jem has got his commission - in a Goorkha regiment!"

The lady who spoke leant back in her chair, half turning her head, but not looking entirely round in the direction of the only other occupant of the room - a girl of nineteen.

"In a Goorkha regiment, Aunt Anna?" repeated the girl; "what is that? It sounds as if he would have to black his face and wear a turban. It suggests curry and gymkhanas (whatever they may be) and pyjamas and bananas and other pickles. A Goorkha regiment."

There was a faint drop in her tone - on the last three words, which to very keen ears might have signified reproach, but the hearer was not keen - merely cunning, which is quite a different matter.

"Yes, dear. They tell me that these Indian regiments are much the best for a young man who is likely to get on. There are so many more chances of promotions and - er - er - distinction."

The girl was standing by the open window, and she turned her head without otherwise moving, looking at the speaker with a pair of exceedingly discriminating eyes.

"Bosh, my dear aunt!" she whispered confidingly to the blind-cord.

"Yes," pursued the lady, with the eager credulity of her first mother, ever ready to believe the last speaker when belief is convenient - "Yes. Sister Cecilia tells me that all the great men began in the Indian Service."

"Oh! I wonder where they finished. Royal Academy - finishing Academy. Regimentals and a gold frame - leaning heroically on a mild-looking cannon with battles in the background."

"Yes, dear," replied Mrs. Agar, who only half understood Dora Glynde at all times; "it is such a good thing for Jem. Such a splendid opportunity, you know!"

"Yes," echoed the girl, with a twist of her humorous lips. "Splendid!"

She had turned again, and was looking out of the window across a soft old lawn where two Wellingtonians towered side by side like sentries. Without glancing in the direction of her companion she knew the expression of Mrs. Agar's face, the direction of her gaze; the very thought in her shallow mind. She knew that Mrs. Agar was sitting with her arms on the little davenport, gazing rapturously at the photograph of an insipid young man with a silk-faced smoking jacket; with clean linen, clean countenance, clean hands, immaculate hair, and a general air of being too weak to be mean.

"Sister Cecilia," went on the elder lady, "seems to know all about it."

It is useless to attempt concealment of the fact that at this juncture Dora Glynde made a face - an honest schoolgirl behind-your-back Face - indicative of supreme scorn for some person or persons unspecified.

Hers was a countenance which lent itself admirably to the purpose, with lips full of humour, and capable, as such lips are, of expressing a great and wonderful tenderness. The face, *du reste*, was that of a healthy, fair-skinned English girl, liable to honest change from pale to pink, according to the dictates of an arbitrary climate. Her eyes were of a dark grey-blue, straightforward and steady, with a shadow of thought in them which made wise people respect her presence. She was not painfully beautiful, like the heroine of a novel - nor abnormally plain, like the antitype who has found her way into fiction, and there (alone) brings all hearts to her feet.

"Is Jem glad?" she asked cheerfully. "Is he thirsting for gore and glory?"

"Oh, delighted! Arthur will be so pleased too. Dear boy, *he* is so interested in soldiers, but of course he could not go into the army! He is too delicate - besides, the life is rough, and the risks are very great."

Mrs. Agar was speaking with her head slightly inclined to one side, and she never raised her adoring eyes from the photograph of the insipid young man. Had she done so she would have seen a look of patient, if comic, resignation come over the face of her youthful companion at the mention of her son's name.

"I will tell mother," said Dora Glynde, purposely ignoring Arthur Agar, whose name was always dragged sooner or later into every conversation. "Fancy Jem in a helmet, or a turban, with his face blacked! All the same, if I were a man I should be a soldier. When does he go - to join his regiment?"

"Oh, almost at once."

The girl winced, quietly, between herself and the blind-cord.

"And in the meantime," she said lightly, "I suppose he is fully engaged in buying swords and guns and bomb-shells, or whatever the Goorkhas use in warfare."

"He is coming home to-morrow for Sunday," replied Jem Agar's stepmother absently. She was thinking of her own son, and therefore did not hear the quick sigh which was almost a gasp; did not note the sudden light in the girl's eyes.

Dora Glynde was rather a solitary-minded young person. The only child of elderly parents, she had never learnt in the nursery to indulge in the indiscretions of confiding girlhood. She had the good fortune to be without a bosom-friend who related her most sacred secrets to other bosom friends and so on, as is the way of maidens. From her father she had inherited a discriminating mind and a most admirable habit of reserve. She was quite happy when alone, which, according to La Bruyère, is a great safeguard against all evil.

She wanted to be alone now, and therefore passed out of the open window with a non-committing "Good-bye, Aunt Anna!"

"Good-bye, dear," replied the lady, awaking suddenly from a reverie. But by the time she had turned round in her chair, the girl was gone.

Dora crossed the lawn, passing between the sentinel pines and crossing the moat by the narrow footbridge. She climbed the railing with all the ease of nineteen years and struck a bee-line across the park. She never raised her eyes from the ground, never paused in her swinging gait, until she reached the brown hush of the beechwood which divided the Rectory garden from the southern extremity of the park.

Having climbed the railing again she sat on a mossy mound at the foot of a huge beech tree. Her manner of doing so subtly indicated that she did not only know the spot, but was in the habit of sitting there, possibly to think. A youthful privilege of doubtful value, for, as we get busier in life we have to do the thinking as we go along.

"Oh!" she muttered, "oh, how awful!"

A new expression had come over her face. She looked older, and all the vivacity had suddenly left her lips.

While she was still sitting there the crisp sound of

footsteps on the fallen leaves approached through the wood. Looking up she saw her father, following the winding path through the spinney towards his home.

A grave man was the Rector of Stagholme in his declining years; hopelessly, wisely pessimistic, with sudden youthful returns of interest in matters literary and theological. As he came he read a book.

Instantly the expression of Dora's face changed. She rose and went towards him, smiling contemptuously towards his lowering gravity. He looked up, gave a little grunt of recognition, and closed his book.

"Father," she said, "I've just heard a piece of news."

"Bad, I suppose."

She laughed.

"Well," she answered, "I suppose we shall survive it. Jem has got his commission, in a Goorkha regiment."

"Goorkha regiment? Nonsense!"

"Aunt Anna has just told me so. She is very pleased, and seems prepared for the - best."

"That is the custom of fools, to be prepared for the best - only."

The Rector gave a despairing shrug of the shoulders. He was a man who allowed himself, after the manner of the ancients with whom he lived mentally, a few gestures. He smoked a very expressive cigarette. He was smoking one at this moment, and threw it away half consumed. This divine was possessed of a rooted conviction that the Almighty made a great mistake whenever He invested temporal power in a woman, whom he was ungallantly inclined to classify under a celebrated dictum of Mr. Carlyle's respecting the population of these happy Isles, who, truth to tell, care not one jot what Mr. Carlyle may think of them.

The Reverend Thomas Glynde and his daughter walked all the way home without exchanging another word. In the Rectory drawing-room they found Mrs. Glynde, small, nervous, worried. She had evidently devoted considerable thought and attention to the preservation of the hot buttered toast. Poor humble little soul, she was quite content to minister to the bodily requirements of her spouse, having long been convinced of the inferiority of her own sex in every respect except a certain limited knowledge of housekeeping matters.

She was vaguely conscious of inferiority to Dora from a literary point of view, and talked with abject humility to her own daughter of all things appertaining to books. But on all other points connected with the child of her old age this quiet little woman was absolute mistress. Years before the Rector had made a great mistake; he had, as the plain-spoken East Burgen doctor put it, made an ass of himself on the matter of a childish illness, thereby imperilling Dora's half-fledged little life. Mrs. Glynde had then, like a diminutive tigress, stood up boldly before her awesome lord and master, saying such things to him that the remembrance of them made her catch her breath even now. From that time forth the Rector was allowed to hold forth on symptoms to his heart's content, to take down from his library shelf a stout misguided book of medical short-cuts to the grave, but nothing more.

He never referred to the asinine business, and in the course of years he forgave the doctor (having in view the fact that that practitioner had been carried away by a right and proper sense of the importance of the case), but he tacitly acknowledged that in the practice of home-administered medical assistance, his knowledge was second to a mother's instinct.

"It appears," he said sharply, while he was stirring his tea, "that Jem Agar has got his commission in a Goorkha regiment."

Now Mrs. Glynde knew more about the organisation of the heavenly bands than of the administration of the Indian army. She did not know whether to rejoice or lament, and having been sharply pulled up - any time during the last twenty years - for doing one or the other in the wrong place, she meekly took soundings.

"What is that, dear?" she inquired.

"The Goorkhas are native Indian soldiers," explained the Rector. "Very good fellows, no doubt. They get all the hard knocks in small frontier wars and none of the half-pence. What the woman can have been thinking of, I don't know."

Mrs. Glynde was anxiously glancing towards Dora, who was nicking the nose of a sportive kitten with the tassel of the tea-cosy.

"And will he go to India?" she asked, with laudable mental grovellings in the mire of her own ignorance.

"Course he will."

"And," added Dora cheerfully, "he will come home covered with glory and medals, with a weakness for strong pickles and hot language - I mean hot pickles and strong language."

"But," said Mrs. Glynde rather breathlessly, "are they never stationed in England?"

"No - never," replied her husband snappishly.

Mrs. Glynde had a pink patch on each cheek - precisely on the spot whore two such patches had appeared years ago when the doctor spoke so strongly. Those patches were maternal, and only appeared when Dora's affairs, spiritual or temporal, were concerned.

"I don't know," put in Dora again, "but I have a sort of lurking conviction that Jem will have to wear a turban and red morocco boots."

"But," pursued Mrs. Glynde, with that courage which cometh with a red patch on either cheek, "I always thought these Indian regiments were meant for people who are badly off."

The Rector gave a short laugh.

"You are not so very far wrong, my dear," he admitted. "And no one can say that Jem is badly off. He will be very rich some day."

The Rector assumed an air of superior discretion, to which he usually treated his women-folk when he thought fit to consider that they were touching on matters beyond their jurisdiction.

"Some more tea, please, mother," put in Dora appropriately. "Excuse my appetite. I suppose it is the autumn air."

There was a short silence, during which Mrs, Glynde sought to propitiate her angered spouse with sodden toast and a second brew of tea.

"I always said," observed the Rector at last, "that your cousin was a fool."

And in some indefinite way Mrs. Glynde felt that she was once more responsible.

CHAPTER VI

FOR HIS COUNTRY

Shall I forget on this side of the grave?
I promise nothing; you must wait and see.

From the train arriving at East Burgen station at eight o'clock that same evening there alighted a youth who seemed suddenly to have taken manhood upon his shoulders. He stood on the platform and pointed out to a porter, who called him Master James, a large Gladstone bag and a new sword-case.

Although he could have carried the luggage under one arm and the porter under the other, he carefully refrained from offering to convey anything except his own walking-stick. Such is the force of education. This boy had been brought up to expect service. He was to be served all his life, and so the sword-case had to be left to the porter whom he envied.

During the journey down - between the farthest-removed stations - the sword had flashed more than once in the dim light of the carriage lamp. Ah! those first swords! Not Toledo nor Damascus can produce their equal in after years.

The porter, honest father of two private soldiers of the

line himself, saw it all - at once. He carried the sword-case with an exaggerated reverence and forbore from remark just then. Afterwards, beneath the station-lamp, he looked at the shilling - the first of its kind from that quarter - with a pathetic, meaning smile.

It was Saturday night. The streets of East Burgen were rather crowded, and Jem Agar - with elbows well in and the whip at the regulation angle across old Lasher's face, who could not help squinting at the pendant thong - shouted to the country-folk in a new voice of mighty deep register.

He carried his boyish head stiffly, and had for ever discarded a turn-down collar. At first he kept old Lasher at a respectful distance, asking in a somewhat curt and business-like manner after the stables. Then gradually, as they bowled along the country road in the familiar hush of an April evening, he thawed, and proceeded to vouchsafe to that steady coachman a series of very interesting details of military matters in general and the Indian army in particular.

"Well, I'm sure, Mas - sir," opined Mr. Lasher at length; "if there's any one as has got into his right rut, so to speak, in this world, it's you. I always said you was a born soldier."

"Ah - then you've heard that I've got my commission?" inquired Jem airily, as if he had had many such in bygone years.

"Oh yes, sir! Miss Dora it was that told me."

Somehow this caused a little silence.

Truth to tell, Dora had lost her rank as the most beautiful and accomplished maiden in Christendom. This situation was at that moment occupied by a young person hight Evelina Louisa Barmond, sister to Billy Barmond of the Hundred and second, a veteran fellow-soldier and comrade who had jumped five feet six at the Sandhurst sports a year before. Miss Evelina Louisa was twenty-four, five years Dora's senior, and only three years and two months older than Jem Agar himself. He had spoken to her twice, and thought about her in the intervals allowed by such weighty matters as uniform and the new sword, which, however, required almost constant consideration at that time.

"Well," said Jem, with exaggerated nonchalance, "I am afraid I should never be fit for anything else."

Whereat Lasher laughed and touched his hat. He made it a rule to salute a joke in that manner, either from a general respect for humour, or looking at it in the light of a mental gratuity offered by his betters.

"There's one thing you can do, Master Jem, sir - leastwise, which you can do as well as any man in the British army," he said, with pardonable pride, "and that is sit a 'orse."

"Thanks to you, Lasher," Jem was kind enough to say with a flourish of his whip.

The dignity was now ebbing fast, and by the time that the clever little cob swung round the gate-post into the avenue of Stagholme, Jem and Lasher were fully re-established on the old familiar footing.

There was a bright moon overhead, and at the end of

the avenue beyond the dip where the lake gleamed mysteriously, the gables and solid towers of Stagholme stood peacefully confessed.

Jem Agar was firmly convinced that England only contained one Stagholme, and perhaps he was right. Six miles from the nearest station, the great house stands self-sufficient, self-contained. The moat, now dry and cultivated, is still traceable, and requires bridging in two places. Surrounded by vast park-like meadowland, where huge trees guard against cutting wind or prying modern journalistic instinct, the house is only approached by a private road.

Inside the gates of this road there is something ancient and feudal in the very scent of the air. The tones of the big bell striking the hour over the wide portico die away over the lands that still belong to Stagholme, despite the vicissitudes through which all ancient families run.

Jem, however, whose childhood and youth had been passed amidst companions with names as good as his, had learnt long ago to keep his pride to himself. He was Jem Agar, and the family name seemed somehow to belong exclusively to his father still, although that thorough old sportsman had lain for three years and more beneath the quiet turf of the little churchyard within his own park gates.

As he pulled up at the door this was thrown open, and within its frame of light he saw the gracious form of his stepmother waiting to welcome him. Behind her, in the shadow, and amidst the decoration of staghorns, ancient pike and hanger, loomed a tall dark figure startlingly in keeping with the semi-monastic architecture of the house. This was Sister Cecilia. She was always thus - behind Mrs. Agar, with clasped hands and a vaguely approving smile, as if Mrs. Agar conferred a benefit upon suffering humanity by the mere act of existing.

A slightly bored expression came into Jem's patient eyes. It was not that he had very much in common with his stepmother, although he had an honest affection for her; but he instinctively disliked Sister Cecilia and all her works. These latter were of the class termed "good." That is to say, this lady, the spinster daughter of a former rector in the neighbourhood, considered that the earthly livery of a marvellous black bonnet which was almost a cap, and quite hideous, justified a shameless interference in the most intimate affairs of her neighbours, rich and poor.

Under the cover of charity she committed a thousand social sins. She constituted herself mother-confessor to all who were weak enough to confide in her or seek her advice, and in soul she was the most arrant time-server who ever flattered a rich woman.

Jem distrusted her soft and "holy" ways, more especially her speech, which had the lofty condescension of the saved towards the damned in prospective. In his calmly commanding way he had, months before, forbidden Dora Glynde to kiss Sister Cecilia, because that ostentatiously virtuous person was in the habit of kissing the maids when she met them; and he maintained that this Christian practice, if very estimable theoretically, was socially an insult either to the mistress or the maid.

In view of the important changes in his own life which

were about to supervene, that is to say, firstly, his departure for India, and secondly, his coming of age before he could hope to return from that land of promise, he had counted on a quiet evening with his mother. Moreover, he was vaguely conscious of the fact that a right-minded person would have carefully abstained from accepting the most pressing invitation to form a third that evening.

In view of this Jem Agar had recourse to the last refuge of the simple. He retired within himself, and, so to speak, shut the door. He had dined with these women before, and knew that the conversation would follow its usual mazy course through a forest of cross-questions upon all subjects, and notably upon those intimate matters which were essentially his own business.

Sister Cecilia, good mistaken soul that she was, tried her best. She was lively in a Sunday-school-tea style. She was by turns tender and warlike as occasion seemed to demand; but no scrap or tittle of personal information did she extract from Jem, stiffly on guard behind his high collar. Mrs. Agar was excited and failed utterly to follow the wiser footsteps of her bosom friends. She talked such arrant nonsense about India, the Goorkhas, and matters military, that more than once Jem glanced at the imperturbable servants with misgiving.

The next day was Sunday, and after morning service Jem eagerly accepted an invitation to have supper at the Rectory after evening church. Sister Cecilia was staying from Saturday till Monday, which alone was sufficient reason for this young soldier to pass his last evening in Stagholme under another than his own historic roof. With her in the house he knew that the chances of serious conversation were small; for she encouraged such topics as the possibility of sending fresh eggs packed in lime to the Goorkhas of his prospective half-company. So Jem retired within himself, and finally left England without having said many things which should have been said between stepmother and son.

At the Rectory he found a very different atmosphere - that air of cheerful intellectuality which comes from the presence of cultivated men and women.

The Rector held strong views on the rare virtue of minding one's own business, and in loyalty to such, deemed it right to refrain from mentioning his opinion as to the wisdom of selecting a native branch of the military service for the heir to Stagholme.

The supper passed pleasantly enough in the discussion of general topics all bordering on the great question they had at heart. They were like people seeking for each other in the dark around the edge of a pit - the pit being India. Dora, and Dora alone, laughed and treated matters lightly. Mrs. Glynde blundered several times, and stepping backwards over an abyss of years, called the new soldier "darling" more than once. Twice she required helping out by Dora, and on the second occasion something was said which Jem remembered afterwards with a stolid British memory.

"Jem," said the girl, buttering a biscuit with a light hand, "you should write a diary. All great men write diaries which their friends publish afterwards."

"I do not think," replied Jem, with that contempt for

the pen which the possession of a new sword ever justifies, "that writing a diary is much in my line."

"Ah, you can never tell till you try. Of course it would not be published straight off. Some literary person would be hired to cross the t's and dot the i's."

There was a little pause. Dora glanced at Jem Agar, and something made him say:

"All right. I'll try."

"Who knows?" said the Rector, with a smile of indulgent affection. "There may be great literary capacity lying dormant in Jem. The worst of a diary is that one may come to look at it in after years, when one finds a very different story has been written from what one intended to write."

"Oh," said Dora, lightly skipping over the chasm of gravity, "that is Providence. We must blame Providence for these little *contretemps*. Some one must be blamed, and Providence obviously does not mind."

Jem laughed - somewhat lamely; but still it was a laugh. Supper was despatched somehow - as last meals are. Some of us never forget the flavour of those cups of tea gulped down in the gorgeous steamer-saloon while the stewards get the hand luggage on board. It was a late meal on Sunday evening at the Rectory, and the servants soon followed their betters into the drawing-room for prayers.

Then the Rector lighted his last cigarette, and Mrs. Glynde began to show symptoms of a patch of pink in either cheek.

At last Jem rose - awkwardly - in the midst of a sally from Dora, who seemed afraid to stop speaking.

"Must be going," he said; and he shook hands with the Rector.

Mrs. Glynde, with nervous deliberation, kissed him and squeezed his hand jerkily.

"Dora - will open the door for you," she said, with an apprehensive glance towards her husband, who, however, showed no inclination to move from his chair.

Dora not only opened the door, but left it open, and walked with him across the lawn towards the stile. When they reached it there was a little pause. He vaulted over and she quietly followed - without his proffered assistance.

Then at last Jem spoke.

"You don't seem to care!" he said gruffly - with his new voice.

"Oh, *don't!*" she whispered imploringly.

And they walked on beneath the murmuring trees where the yellow moonlight stole in and out between the trunks. It was not cheerful. For when Nature joins her sadness to the sad libretto of life she usually breaks a heart or two. Fortunately for us we mostly act our tragedies in the wrong scenery - the scenery that was painted for a comedy.

"I don't understand it," said the girl at length.

"I suppose it is in order to save money for Arthur."

"If I don't, go," replied Jem, "it will be a question of letting Stagholme."

Dora knew of the ancient horror of such a necessity, handed down from one Agar to another, like a family tradition. Moreover, women seem to respect men who have some simple creed and hold to it simply. Are they not one of our creeds themselves, though by seeking for rights instead of contenting themselves with privileges, some of them try to make atheists of us?

"So," she said nevertheless, "you are being sacrificed to Arthur!"

He answered nothing, but he had forgotten for ever Miss Evelina Louisa Barmond.

"When do you go?" asked Dora suddenly, with something in her voice which no one had ever heard before. She was startled at it herself.

He waited until the soft old church bell finished striking ten, then he answered:

"To-morrow!"

They had reached the farthest limit of the wood and stood at the park railing.

"Then -," she paused, and seemed to collect herself as if for a leap; "then good-bye, Jem!"

He took the outstretched hand; his large grasp seemed to swallow it up.

"Good-bye!" he said.

He climbed the rail without agility, paused for a moment, and the moonlight happened to gleam on his face through the gently waving branches as he looked down at her in dumb distress.

Then he turned and walked away across the shimmering grass.

A few minutes later Dora re-entered the drawing room. Her father and mother were seated close together, closer than she had seen them for years. Mrs. Glynde was pale, with two scarlet patches.

Dora collected her belongings, preparatory to going to bed.

"Jem," she said quietly, "is absurdly proud of his new honours. It affects his chin, which has gone up exactly one inch."

Then she went to bed.

CHAPTER VII

ON THE ROOF OF THE WORLD

The more a man has in himself, the less he will want from other people.

"Here - hi!"

As no one replied to this summons either, by voice or approach, the young man subsided into occupied silence.

He was a very large young man, with a fair moustache which looked almost flaxen against the deep tan of his face. This last, like the rest of him, was ludicrously typical of that race which has wandered farther than the Jews, and has hitherto managed, like them, to retain a few of its characteristics. The Anglo-Saxonism of this youth was almost aggressive. It lurked in the neat droop of moustache, which was devoid of that untidy suggestion of a beer-mug characterising the labial adornment of a northern flaxen nation of which we wot. It shone calmly in the glance of a pair of reflectively deep blue eyes - it threw itself at one from the pockets of an old tweed jacket worn in conjunction with regulation top-boots and khaki breeches.

Moreover, it gave birth to a quiet sense of being as

　　　Henry Seton Merriman

good as any one else, and possibly better, which sat without conceit on his brow.

It would seem that he really did not want to be answered just then, for he did not raise a voice accustomed to dominate the clatter of horses' feet, nor did he pass any comment on the carelessness or criminal absence of some person or persons unknown.

He merely took up his pen again, and proceeded to handle that mighty weapon with an awkwardness suggestive of a greater skill with another instrument only less powerful. He was seated on two reversed buckets, pyramidally balanced, at a small table which had the air of wide capabilities in some other sphere of usefulness. There was a weird cunning in the legs of this table indicative of subtle change into a camp-bed or possibly a canoe.

The writing materials consisted of a vaseline bottle (fourpenny size) full of ink, and two weary pieces of blotting-paper. The paper upon which he was writing had a travelled and somewhat jaundiced air, the penholder was of gold. In the furniture of the tent, as in the canvas thereof, there was that mournful suggestion of better days which is held to be a virtue in furnished apartments. But over all there hovered that sense of well-scrubbed cleanliness which comes from the touch of a native military servant. An indulgence in this habit of rubbing and scrubbing was indeed accountable for much dilapidation; for that silent little Ghoorka man, Ben Abdi, had rubbed and scrubbed many things not intended by an ingenious camp-furnisher for such treatment. James Edward Makerstone Agar was engaged in the compilation of a diary, which volume there is reason to believe is still preserved in a woman's jewel drawer.

It has not run through any editions - indeed, no compositor's finger has up to this time defiled its pages. This, in fact, was one of those literary works, ground slowly out from the millstones of the brain, of which the style fails to please the taste of the present day. To catch the fancy of a slang-loving and thoughtless generation the writer must throw off his works. This is an age of "throwing off," and it is to be presumed that future ages will throw the result away. One must be brilliant, shallow, slightly unpleasant and very unwholesome, to acquire nowadays that best of all literary reputations which leaveth a balance at one's bank.

J.E.M. Agar - or "Jem" as his friends call him to his face and his servants behind his back - Jem Sahib to wit - was no Pepys. His literary style was disjointed, heavy, and occasionally illiterate. This last peculiarity, by the way, is of no consequence nowadays, but it is mentioned here for ulterior motives. In the pages of this little black-bound volume there were no scintillating thoughts scribbled there with suspicious neatness of diction, such as one finds in the diaries of great men who, it would seem, are not above post-mortem vanity. The diary was a chronicle of solid facts - Jem being essentially solid and a man of the very plainest facts.

Speaking as an impartial critic, one would incline to the opinion that Agar devoted too much thought to his work - in strong contrast, perhaps, to the literary tendency of his day. He nibbled the leisure end of his penholder too much, and allowed the business extremity thereof to dry in inky conglomeration. The result was a distinct sense of labour in the style of the work. After having called in vain, perhaps for assistance, the scribe returned to the contemplation of his latest effort. The book was one of Letts's diaries, three days in a page, which are in themselves fatal to a finished style of literature. There is always too much to say or too little. One's thoughts never fit the rhomboid apportioned by Mr. Letts for their accommodation. Great men who have thoughts when the diary is handy do not, of course, patronise Letts, because he could not be expected to know when there would be a sunset likely to stir up poetic reflections, or a moonrise comparable with the cold light cast by some unsympathetic young woman's eyes upon the poet's life.

For such men, however, as Agar, Mr. Letts is a guardian angel. The space is there, and facts must be forthcoming to fill it. Agar was, and is still - thank Heaven - a conscientious man. He had promised to keep this diary and keep it he did. And surely he hath his reward - remembering the jewel drawer.

At the moment under consideration he was filling in yesterday's rhomboid, and paused at the conclusion of the following remarks:

"*Seven* A.M. Turned out, and shot a Ghilzai. Saw him sneaking up the valley. Long shot - should put it down at a hundred and seventy-five yards. Hit him in the stom - abd - chest. Looked like rain until two o'clock. Then cleared up. Walter caught a mongoose and brought him in with much triumph. He got conceited afterwards and slept on my bed till kicked off by Ben Abdi. I see it's Sunday. Church four hundred odd miles away."

This, my masters, is not the stuff to quote *in extenso*, and yet in its day this diary was cried over - before it was put away in the jewel drawer. Truly women are strange - one can never tell how a thing will present itself to them. Honest Jem Agar, nibbling his penholder and jerking these lucid observations out of his military brain by mere force of discipline, never suspected the heart that was in it all - that minute particle of himself that lay in the blot in the corner carefully absorbed by the exhausted blotting-paper.

"Sunday, egad!" he muttered, leaning his arms on the cunning table, and gazing out across the pine-clad valley that lay below him in a deep blue haze.

He stared into the haze, and there he saw those whom he called "his people" walking across a neat English park toward a peaceful little English church. To them came presently a young person; a young person clad in pink cotton, who walked with a certain demure sureness of tread, as if she knew her own mind and other things besides. Her path came into the park from the left, and among the trees into which it disappeared behind her there stood the red chimneys of a long low house.

Suddenly these visions vanished before something more tangible in the haze of the valley. This was the flutter of a dirty white rag which seemed to come and go among the fir trees.

Jem Agar rose from his temporary seat and walked to the door of the tent - exactly two strides. A rifle lay against the canvas, and this he took up, slowly cocking it without taking his eyes from the belt of fir trees across the valley.

Presently he threw the rifle up and fired instantaneously. He had been musketry instructor in his time and held views upon quick firing. The smoke rose lazily in the ambient air, and he saw a figure all fluttering rags and flying turban running down the slope away from him. At the same moment there was a crashing volley, followed by two straggling reports. The figure stopped, seemed to hesitate, and then slowly subsided into the grass.

Agar put his head out of the tent and saw half a company of Goorkhas, keen little sportsmen all standing in line at the edge of the plateau, reloading.

This was the force at the disposal of Major J. E. M. Agar, at that time occupying and holding for Her Majesty the Queen of England and Empress of India a very advanced position on the northern frontier of India. And in this manner he spent most of his days and some of his nights. In addition to the plain Major he had several other titles attached to his name at that time, indicative of duties real and imaginary. He was "deputy assistant" several things and "acting" one or two; for in military titles one begins in inverse ratio in a large way, and ends in something short.

Jem Agar was thought very highly of by almost all concerned, except himself, and it had not occurred to him to devote much thought to this matter. He was one of the very few men to whom a senior officer or a pretty girl could say, "You are a nice man and a clever fellow," without doing the least harm. Men who thought such things of themselves laughed at him behind his back, and wondered vaguely why he got promotion. It never occurred to them to reflect that "old Jem" invariably acquitted himself well in each new position thrust upon him by a persistently kind fortune; they contented themselves with an indefinite conviction that each severally could have done better, as is the way of clever young men. One of the many mysteries, by the way, which will have to be cleared up in a busy hereafter is that appertaining to brilliant boys, clever undergraduates, and gifted young men. What becomes of them? There are hundreds at school at this moment - we have it from their own parents; hundreds more at Oxford and Cambridge - we have it from themselves. In a few years they will be absorbed in a world of men very much inferior to themselves (by their own showing), and will be no more seen.

Jem Agar had never been a clever boy. He was not a clever man. But - and mark ye this - he knew it. The result of this knowledge was that he did what he could in the present with the present, and did not indefinitely postpone astonishing the universe, as most of us do, until some future date.

At this time he was banished, as some would take it. Banished to the top of a pass which was nought else than a footway between two empires. Forty miles from men of his own race, this man was one of those who either have no thoughts or no wish to impart them; for this racial solitude, which is an emotion fully explored by many in India, in no way affected his nerves. Some say that they get jumpy, others aver that they begin to lose their national characteristics and develop barbarous proclivities, while one Woods-and-Forests man known to some of us resigned because he had a buzzing in the head during the long solitary, silent evenings.

Major Agar made no statements on this point, though

he listened with sympathy to the assertions of others. If the sympathy were subtly mingled with non-comprehensive wonder, the seeker after a purer form of commiseration attributed the alloy to natural density, and turned elsewhere.

Accompanied by a handful of Goorkhas, Major J. E. M. Agar had occupied the key to this narrow pass for more than a week, vaguely admiring the scenery, illustrating upon living "running deer" in turbans his views upon quick firing to his diminutive soldiers, who worshipped him as second only to the gods, and possessing his soul with that trustful patience which is rapidly becoming old-fashioned and effete.

During that same week the newspapers at home had been very busy with his name. Some had gone so far as to lay before a greedy public a short and succinct account of his life, compiled from the Army List and a journalistic imagination, finishing the record on the Monday, six days previously, with the usual three-line regret that England should in future be compelled to limp along the path to glory without the assistance of so brilliant a young officer.

Such a word as brilliant had never been coupled with the name of Jem even by his best friend in earnest or his worst enemy in irony. Such sarcasm were too shallow to be worth sounding even in disparagement. But we never know what an obituary notice may bring. Not only had he been endowed with many virtues, manly qualities, and the record of noble deeds, but more substantial honours had been heaped upon his fallen crest or pinned upon his breathless bosom. To some of his distant countrymen he was the proud possessor of the Victoria Cross , awarded him post-mortem in the heat of obituary enthusiasm by more than one local paper. To others he was held up by what is called a Representative Press as a second Crichton. And all this because he was dead. Such is glory.

All unconscious of these honours, honest Jem Agar sat in his little tent, nibbling the end of his penholder - the gift, by the way, of his father - and wishing that he had bought a Letts's diary with six days in a page instead of three.

CHAPTER VIII

RELIEVED

Well waited is well done.

"Here - hi!"

This time some one heard him, and that small, silent man, Ben Abdi, stood in the doorway of the tent at attention.

"Are you keeping a good look-out down the valley?" asked Major Agar.

"Ee yess, sar."

"No signs of any one?"

"No, sar."

Agar shut up the diary, which book Ben Abdi had been taught to regard as strictly official, laid it aside, and passed out of the tent, the little Goorkha following close upon his heels with a quick intelligent interest in his every movement which somehow suggested a dusky and faithful little dog.

For some moments they stood thus on the edge of the

small plateau, the big man in front, the little one behind - alert, with twinkling, beady eyes. Behind them towered a bleak grey slope of bare rock, like a cliff set back at a slight angle, so treeless, so smooth was the face of it. In front the great blue-shadowed valley lay beneath them, stretching away to the south, until in a distant haze the sharp hills seemed to close in and cut it short.

Perched thus, as it were, upon the roof of the world, these two men looked down upon it all with a calm sense of possession, and to him of the dominant race standing there some thousands of miles from his native land - alone - master of this great stretch of an alien shore, there must have come some passing thought of the strangeness of it all.

There was something wrong - he knew that. His orders had been to press forward and occupy this little ridge, which was vaguely marked on the service maps as Mistley's Plateau, named after an adventurous soul, its discoverer. He had been instructed to hold this against all comers, and if possible to prevent communication between the two valleys, connected only by this narrow pass. All this Agar had carried out to the letter; but some one else had failed somewhere.

"It will be three days at the most," his chief had said, "and the main body of the advance guard will join you!"

Jem Agar had been in occupation a week, and it seemed that he and his little band of men were forgotten of the world. Still this soldier held on, saying nothing to his men, writing his intensely practical diary, and trusting as a soldier should to the *Deus ex machina* who finally allows discipline to triumph. He looked down into the valley, piercing the shimmer of its hazes with his gentle blue eyes, looking to his chief, who had said, "In three days I will join you."

It was not the first time that Agar and the little non-commissioned native officer, Ben Abdi, had stood thus together. They had taken their stand in this same spot in the keen air of the early morning, with the white frost crystallising the stones around them; in the glow of midday; and when the moon, hanging over the sharp-pointed hills, cast the valley into an opaque shade dark and fathomless as the valley of death.

Scanning the distant hills, Agar presently raised his eyes, noting the position of the sun in the heavens.

"Have you tried the heliograph a second time this morning?" he asked without looking round, which informality of manner warmed the little soldier's heart.

"Yes, sar. Three times since breakfast."

It was the first time that Ben Abdi had found himself in a position of some responsibility, in immediate touch with one of the white-skinned warriors from over seas whose methods of making war had for him all the mystery and the infinite possibilities of a religion. This silent looking out for relief partook in some small degree of the nature of a council of war. Jem Sahib and himself were undoubtedly the chiefs of this expeditionary force, and to whom else than himself, Ben Abdi, should the Major turn for counsel and assistance? The little Goorkha preferred, however, that it should be thus; that Agar Sahib should say nothing, merely allowing him to stand silent three paces behind.

He was a modest little man, this Goorkha, and knew the limit of his own capabilities, which knowledge, by the way, is not always to be found in the hearts of some of us boasting a fairer skin. He knew that for hard fighting, snugly concealed behind a rock at two hundred yards, or in the open, with cunning bayonet or swinging kookery, he was as good as his fellows; but for strategy, for the larger responsibilities of warfare, he was well pleased that his superior officer should manage these affairs in his quiet way unaided.

During a luncheon more remarkable for heartiness of despatch than delicacy of viand, James Edward Makerstone Agar devoted much thought to the affairs of Her Imperial Majesty the Empress of India. After luncheon he lighted a cheroot, threw himself on his bed, and there reflected further. Then he called to him Ben Abdi.

"No more promiscuous shooting," he said to him. "No more volley firing at a single Ghilzai or a stray Bhutari. It seems that they do not know we are here, as we are left undisturbed. I do not want them to know - understand? If you see any one going along the valley, send two men after him; no shooting, Ben Abdi."

And he pointed with his cheroot towards the evil-looking curved knife which hung at the Goorkha's side.

Ben Abdi grinned. He understood that sort of business thoroughly.

Then followed many technical instructions - not only technical in good honest English, but interlarded with words from a language which cannot be written with our alphabet for the benefit of such as love details of a realistic nature.

The result of this council was that sundry little dusky warriors were busy clambering about the rocky slope all that day and well into the short hill-country evening, working in twos and threes with the *alacrity* of ants.

Jem Agar, in his own good time, was proceeding to further fortify, as well as circumstances allowed, the position he had been told to hold until relief should come. In addition to the magic of the master's eye he lent the assistance of his strong right arm, laying his lithe weight against many a rock which his men could not move unaided. By the evening the position was in a fairly fortified state, and, after a copious dinner in the chill breeze that rushed from the mountain down to the valley after sunset, he walked placidly up and down at the edge of the plateau, watching, ever watching, but with calmness and no sign of anxiety.

Such it is to be an Englishman - the product of an English public school and country life. Thick-limbed, very quiet; thick-headed if you will! - that is as may be - but with a nerve of iron, ready to face the last foe of all - Death, without so much as a wink.

To his ear came at times the low cautious cry of some night-bird sailing with heavy wing down to the haunt of mouse or mole; otherwise the night was still as only mountain night-seasons are. Far down below him, the jungle and forest were rustling with game and beasts of prey seeking their meat from God, but the larger beasts of India, unlike their African brethren, move in silence, stealthy yet courageous; and the distance was too great for the quickly stifled cry of the victim of panther or tiger to reach him.

When the moon rose he made the round of his pickets - a matter of ten minutes - and then to bed.

On the morning of the ninth day he thought he detected signs of uneasiness in the faces of the men. He found their keen little visages ever turned towards him, watching his every movement, noting the play of every feature. So in his simplicity he practised a simple diplomacy. He hummed to himself as he went his rounds and while he sat over his diary. He only knew one song - "A Warrior Bold" - which every mess in India associated with old Jem Agar, for no evening was considered complete without the Major's one ditty if he were present. He had stood up and roared it in many strange places, quite without sentiment, without self-consciousness, without afterthought. He never thought it a matter of apology that he should have failed to learn another song. The smile with which many ladies of his acquaintance sat down to play the accompaniment *by heart* conveyed nothing to him. He did not pretend to be a singer - he knew that one song, and if they liked it he would sing it. Moreover, they did like it, and that was why they asked for it. It did some of them good to see honest Jem get on his legs and shout out, in a very musical voice, with perfect truth to air, what seemed to be a plain statement of his creed of life.

So, far up on Mistley Plateau, nine thousand feet above the level of the sea, Jem Agar advised his little dark-visaged fighters, *sotto voce*, while he puzzled over his diary, that his love had golden hair, with eyes so blue and heart so true, that none with her compared; moreover, that he didn't care if death were nigh,

Henry Seton Merriman

because he had fought for love, and for love would die.

It was not very deep or very subtle, but it served the purpose. It kept up the hearts of his handful of warriors, who, in common with their chief, had something child-like and simple in their honest, sporting souls.

Shortly after tiffin Ben Abdi came to the Major's tent, speaking hurriedly in his own tongue.

One of the men had seen the sunlight gleam on white steel far down in the valley. He had seen it several times - a long spiral flash, such as the sun would make on a fixed bayonet carried over the shoulder. Such a flash as this will carry twenty miles through a clear atmosphere; the spot pointed out by the sharp-eyed Goorkha was not more than ten miles distant. They stood in a group, this isolated little band, and gazed down into the depth below them. They gazed in vain for some time, then a little murmur of excitement told that the sun had glinted again on burnished steel. This time there were several flashes close together. These were men marching with fixed bayonets through an enemy's country.

"Heliograph," said Agar quietly, without taking his eyes from the spot far down in the valley; and soon the little mirror was flashing out its question over the vale. After a few anxious moments the answering gleam sprang to life among the trees far below. Agar gave a quick little sigh of relief - that was all.

Then followed a short conversation flickered over ten miles of space.

"Are you beset?" asked the Valley,

"No," replied the Hill.

"Is the enemy in sight?"

"No," replied the Mountain, again, with a sharp click.

"Are you all well?" flashed from below.

"Yes," from above.

Then the "Good-bye," and the glimmer of the bayonets began again.

Two hours later Major Agar drew his absurd little force in line, and thus they received the relieving column, grimly conscious of dangers past but not forgotten.

At the head of the new-comers rode a little man with a prominent chin and a long drooping nose; such a remarkable-looking little man that the veriest tyro at physiognomy would have turned to look at him again. His black eyes, beaming with intelligence, moved so quickly beneath the steady lashes that it was next to an impossibility to state what he saw and what he failed to see.

He returned Agar's salute hurriedly, with a preoccupied air. He wore a quiet uniform tunic almost hidden by black braiding, a pith helmet which had seen brighter days and likewise fouler, and the leg that he threw over his horse's head was cased in riding trousers and a neat little top-boot of brown leather.

He slipped from the saddle with a litheness which contrasted strangely with his closely cropped grey hair and white moustache and Imperial. He walked towards Agar's tent after the manner of one who had sat in the saddle for many hours. His spurs clanked with a sharp, business-like ring, and his every movement had that neat finish which indicates the soldier born and bred.

Wheeling round he faced Agar, who had followed him with a more leisurely gait based on longer legs, looking up keenly into the quiet fair face. Turning he shot his sword home into its scabbard with a click.

"Thank God," he said, "you're safe!"

Agar awaited for further observations. This was not the man whom he had expected, but another, far greater, far higher up in the military scale - a man whom he had only met once before, and that at an official reception.

Seeing that his guest was unbuckling his sword, he presumed that the task of continuing this conversation lay with himself.

"M' yes!" he replied, rubbing his pannikin out clean with the corner of a towel, and proceeding to mix some brandy and water; "why?"

"Why!" answered the little man scornfully, "WHY! damn it, sir, Stevenor's command has been cut off by the enemy in force - massacred to a man. That is why I say 'Thank God, you're safe!' It is more than I expected."

CHAPTER IX

RE-CAST

Our deeds still travel with us from afar,
And what, we have been makes us what we are,

There was a momentary pause; then Major Agar spoke.

"In that case," he observed, "the British force occupying this country for the last week has consisted of myself and thirty Goorkhas."

"Precisely so! And it was by the merest chance that I found out that you were here. It was only guesswork at the best. A bazaar report reached me that poor old Stevenor had been cut to pieces. I hate blaming a dead man, but I really don't know what he can have been about. He made some hideous mistake somewhere. We buried him yesterday. On hearing the report, I thought it better to come up myself, having a little knowledge of the country. Brought two companies, and half a squadron to act as scouts. We reached Barkoola yesterday, and found the poor chaps as they had fallen. And some of those carpet-warriors at home say that a black man can't fight! Can't he! Not so much brandy this time, please. Yes, fill it up."

Agar set the regulation water-bottle down on his

Henry Seton Merriman

gifted table.

"I have the Devil's own luck!" he murmured. "While they were burying I missed you from among the officers; and then it struck me that you might have got away before the disaster. We counted the men, and found thirty-four short, so we came on here. By God! what a chap Mistley was! We came here without a check. His maps are perfect!"

"Yes," admitted Agar, "that man knew his business!"

There was something in his tone that might have been envy or perhaps mere admiration; for this man knew himself to be inferior in many ways to him who had first crossed the mountain pass on which he stood.

"The worst of it is," went on the great officer, "that you are telegraphed home as killed."

He paused on the last word, watching its effect. It would seem that, behind the busy black eyes, there was the beginning of a thought hatched within the grey close-cut head which, *en fait de têtes,* was without its rival in the Empire.

"That is soon remedied," opined the Major with a cheerful laugh.

"Ye - es!"

The great man was thoughtfully rubbing his chin with the tips of the first and second fingers, drawing in his under lip at the same time, and apparently taking pleasure in the rasping sound caused by the friction over the shaven chin.

There is usually something written in the human countenance - some single virtue, vice, or quality which dominates all petty characteristics. Most faces express weakness - the faces that pass one in the streets. Some are the incarnation of meanness, some pleasanter types verge on sensuality. The face of the man who sat watching Agar expressed indomitable, invincible determination, and *nothing else*. It was the face of one who was ready to sacrifice any one, even himself, to a single all-pervading purpose. In this respect he was a splendid commander, for he was as nearly heartless as men are made.

The big fair Englishman who had occupied Mistley's Plateau for a week, exactly one hundred and seventy miles from assistance of any description, and in the heart of the enemy's country, smiled down at his companion with a simple wonder.

"Got something up your sleeve, sir?" he inquired softly, for he knew somewhat of his superior officer's ways.

"Yes!" replied the other curtly. "A trump card!"

He continued to look at Jem Agar with a cold and calculating scrutiny, as a jockey may look at his horse or a butcher at living meat.

"It's like this," he said. "You're dead. I want you to stay dead for a little while - say six months to a year!"

Agar seated himself on the corner of the table, which creaked under the weight of his spare muscular person, and then, true to his cloth, he awaited further orders; true to his nature, he waited in silence.

After a short pause the other proceeded to explain.

"You frontier men," he said, "are closely watched; we know that. There will be great rejoicing over there, in Northern Europe, over this mishap to Stevenor, although, God knows, he was not a very dangerous man. Not so dangerous as you, Agar. They will be delighted to hear that you are out of the way. Stay out of the way for a year, and during that twelve months you will be able to do more than you could get done in twelve years when you were being watched by them."

"I see," answered Agar quietly. "Not dead, but gone - up country."

"Precisely so; where they certainly will not be on the look-out for you."

The bright black eyes were shining with suppressed excitement. The great man was afraid that his tool would refuse to work under this exacting touch.

"But what about my people?" asked Agar.

"Oh, I will put that right. You see, they have got over the worst of it by this time. It is wonderful how soon people do get over it. They have known it for a week now, and have bought their mourning and all that."

There came a look into Agar's face which the little officer did not understand. We never do understand what we could not feel ourselves, and it is not a matter of wonder that the lesser intelligence should foil the greater in this instance. There was a depth in Jem Agar which was beyond the fathom of his keen-witted companion.

"I am going home," continued General Michael, "almost at once. The first thing I do on landing is to go straight to your people and tell them. We cannot afford to telegraph it. Telegraph clerks are only human, and it is worth the while of the newspapers in these days of large circulation to pay a heavy price for their news. We all know that some items, published *can* only have been bought from the telegraph clerks."

Agar was making a mental calculation.

"That means," he said, "two months before they hear."

The expression on the face of the little man was scarcely human in its heartless cunning.

"Hardly," he answered carelessly. "And when they hear the reason they will admit that the result is worth the sacrifice. It will be the making of you! - and of me!" added the black eyes with a secretive gleam.

"It is," went on the General, "such a chance as only comes once to a man in his lifetime. I wish I had had it at your age."

The voice was a pleasant one, with that ring of friendliness and familiarity which is usually heard in the tones of an educated Jew; for General Michael was that rare combination, a Jew and a soldier.

"I don't like leaving them so long under the mistake," answered Agar, half yielding to authoritative persuasion, half tempted by ambition and a love of adventure. "I don't like it, General. The straight thing would be to telegraph home at once."

In the wavering smile that crossed the dark face there was suggested a fine contempt for the straight thing unaccompanied by some tangible advantage.

"Who are they?" inquired the General almost affectionately. "Who are your people?"

Agar walked to the tent door and looked out. There was some clatter of swords going on outside, and as commander of this post it was his duty to know all that was passing. He turned, and standing in the doorway, quite filling it with his bulk, he answered:

"My father died three years ago. I have a step-mother and a step-brother, that is all - besides friends."

The General stooped to loosen the strap of his spur.

"Of course," he said in that attitude, "I know you are not a married man."

"No."

Beneath the brim of the helmet, which he had not laid aside, the Jew's keen black eyes were watching, watching. But they saw nothing; for there is no one so impenetrable as a man with a clear conscience and a large faith.

"My idea was," continued General Michael, "that two, or at the most three, people besides you and I be let into the secret."

"Three," said Agar, with quiet decision.

"Three?"

"Yes."

The General tacitly allowed this point and passed on with characteristic promptitude to another.

"Are you a man of property?"

"Yes, I inherit my father's place down in Hertfordshire."

"I'll tell you why I ask. There are those beastly lawyers to think of. At your death it is to be presumed that the estate comes to your brother. The legal operations must be delayed somehow. I will see to it," he added in a concise, almost snappish way.

Agar smiled, although he was conscious of a vague feeling of discomfort. He was not a highly sensitive or a nervous man, and this feeling was more than might have been expected to arise from an attendance, as it were, at one's own obituary arrangements. The General seemed to be remarkably well informed on these smaller points, and something prompted Jem Agar to ask him if the idea he had just propounded was a suddenly conceived one.

"No," replied the General with a singular pause.

"No, I once knew a man who did the same thing for a different purpose, but the idea was identical. I do not claim to be the originator."

"And there was no hitch? It was successful?" inquired Agar.

"Yes," replied the older soldier in a far-away voice, as

if he had mentally gone back to the results of that man's deception. "Yes, it was successful. By the way, you say your people live down in Hertfordshire?"

"Yes."

"I once knew a girl - long ago, in my younger days - who married a man called Agar, and went to live in Hertfordshire. The name did not strike me until you mentioned the county. I wonder if the lady is now your step-mother."

"My step-mother's name was Hethbridge," replied Jem Agar.

"The same. How strange!" said the General indifferently. "Well, she has probably forgotten my existence these thirty years. She has one son, you say?"

"Yes, Arthur. He is twenty-three - five years younger than myself."

The shifty black eyes excelled themselves at this moment in rapidity of observation. They seemed to be full of question, of many questions, but none were forthcoming.

"Ah!" said General Michael indifferently. "He is," pursued Jem Agar, "a delicate fellow; does nothing; though I believe he is going to be called to the Bar."

The General, having passed most of his life in India, where men work or else go home, did not take in the full meaning of this; but he was keen as a ferret, and he saw easily that Jem Agar despised his step-brother with that cruel contempt which strong men feel for weak.

"Mother's darling?" he suggested.

"Yes, that is about it," replied Agar. He was too simple, too innately upright and honest to perceive the infinite possibilities opened up by the fact upon which General Michael had pounced.

"In case you decide to accept my offer," the older man went on, "you would wish your stepmother and step-brother to be told?"

"Yes, and one other person."

"Ah, and another person. You could not limit it to two?" urged the General.

"No!" replied Agar with a decision which the other was wise enough to consider final. Moreover, the General omitted to ask the name of this third person, urged thereto by one of those strokes of instinct which indicate the genius of the commander of men.

General Michael, moreover, deemed it prudent to carry the matter no further at that moment. He rose from his seat on the bed, stretched his lithe limbs, and said:

"Well, this won't do! We must get to work. I propose retreating to-morrow morning at daylight."

They passed out of the tent together and proceeded to give their orders, moving in and out among the busy men. There was a subtle difference in their reception which was perhaps patent to both, though neither deemed it necessary to make any comment. Wherever

Agar went the eager little black faces of his Goorkhas met him with a smile or a grin of delight; when General Michael passed by, the dusky features hardened suddenly to a marble stillness, and the beady eyes were all soldier-like attention.

They feared and loved the one because they felt that there was something in him which they could not understand; they feared and hated the other because his nature was nearer to their own, and they defined the evil in it.

Moreover, each had his reputation - that of General Michael dating from the Mutiny; the other, a younger and a cleaner record.

It is considered the proper thing to talk in England of the unvoiced millions of India. No greater mistake could be made. These millions have a voice, but it does not reach to us because they do not raise it. They talk with it among themselves.

They had talked of General Michael for thirty years, and all that there was in him had been discussed to its very dregs. Thus their impenetrable faces hardened when he passed, their shadowy secretive eyes looked beyond him with a vacancy which was not the vacancy of dulness.

CHAPTER X

A LAST THROW

Get place and wealth; if possible, with grace;
If not, by any means get wealth and place.

Daylight broke next morning in a snow-storm, and a thin sprinkling lay over all the hills, clothing them in spotless white.

General Michael was among the first astir, seeing in person to all the details of the retreat. The men looked in vain towards the tent where their late youthful leader had been wont to sit, nibbling the end of his golden pocket-penholder, wrestling manfully in the throes of literary composition.

When at last the order was given to strike tents the faces of the rank and file fell like the face of one man.

Major James Edward Makerstone Agar had simply disappeared. His limited baggage was attached to the smaller belongings of General Michael, and no explanation was offered by that dreaded officer. To him the cold seemed to be a matter of indifference; for he stood about watching every movement of the men with a supreme disregard for the driving snow or the knife-like wind that whistled over the northern scarp.

Henry Seton Merriman

Under his calculating eye they worked to such effect that by nine o'clock the little column was on the downward march. Again General Michael rode through that lone, lorn country lying between India and Russia. Again his melancholy face with keen but hopeless eyes passed through the darksome valleys where, if legend be true, a race as old as his has lived since the children of Abraham set forth to wander over the earth.

For twenty years this man had haunted these vales and hills, seeking, ever seeking, his own aggrandisement and nothing else. Accounted a patriot, he was no patriot; for the homeless blood was mingled in his veins. Held to be a hero by some, he was none; for he hated danger for its own sake, just as some men love it.

But his lines had been cast in this unpleasant place, from whence flight or retreat was rendered almost impossible, by the laws of discipline and the freak of circumstance. Despite his titles, in face of his great reputation, he knew himself to be a failure, and as he rode southward through the mountain barrier that frowns down over India he was conscious of the knowledge that in all human probability he would never look upon this drear land again. His time was up, he was about to be set on the shelf, life was over. And he had all his powers yet - all his marvellous quickness at the mastery of tongues, all the restless energy which had urged him on to overrun the race, to dodge and bore and break his stride instead of holding steadily on the straight course.

He it was who had discovered Jem Agar's talent for this rough, peculiar soldiering of the frontier. He it was to whom the simple-minded young officer had owed promotion after promotion. General Michael had fixed upon Agar as his last hope - his last chance of doing something brilliant in this deathly country, which moved with a slowness that nearly drove him mad.

This last attempt was thrown down like a defiance in the face of Fortune; but still the risk was not his own. It never had been. Men had been sent to their certain death by this sallow-faced commander, for no other object than his own aggrandisement. It would almost seem that a just Providence had ever turned away in loathing from the schemes of this man who would have all and risk nothing.

Should Jem Agar succeed in the dangerous secret mission on which he had been sent by a subtle under-hand pressure of discipline, the glory would never be his. This, under the grasping fingers of General Michael, would never appear to the world as the wonderful individual feat of an intrepid man, but as a masterly stroke of strategy dealt by a great general.

Seymour Michael had long ago found out that Jem Agar was the step-son of the woman whom he had wronged in bygone years. But the name failed to touch his conscience, partly because that conscience was not of much account, and partly because time heals all things, even a sore sense of wrong. Truth to tell, he had not thought much of Anna Agar during the last twenty years, and the mere coincidence that this simple tool should be her step-son was insufficient to deter him from making use of Agar. But with that careful attention to detail which in such a man betrayed innate weakness, he took care to make sure that Jem Agar had learnt nothing of the past from the lips of his father's second wife.

General Michael did not disguise from himself the fact that the mission on which he had despatched Jem Agar was what the life insurance companies call hazardous. But he had lived by the sword, and that mode of gaining a livelihood makes men wondrously indifferent to the lives of others. Moreover, this was in a sense a speciality of his. He was getting hardened to the game, and played it with coolness and precision.

All through that day the little band retreated through an enemy's country, watchful, alert, almost nervous. There were absurdly few of them - a characteristic of that frontier warfare which the sallow, silent leader had waged nearly all his life. And in the evening there was not peace.

Fortune is a playful soul. She keeps men waiting a lifetime, and then, when it is too late, she suddenly opens both her hands. Seymour Michael had waited twenty years for one of those chances of easy distinction which seemed to fall to the lot of all his comrades in arms. This chance was vouchsafed to him on the last evening he ever passed in an enemy's country - when it was too late - when that which he did was no more than was to be expected from a man of his experience and fame.

The little band was attacked at sunset by the victorious savages who had annihilated the advance column three days earlier, and with half the number of men, fatigued and hungry, Seymour Michael beat them back and cut his way to the south. He knew that it was good, and the men knew it. They looked upon this keen-faced little man as something approaching a demi-god; but they had no love for him as they had for Major Agar. The knowledge was theirs that to him their lives were of no account - they were not men, but numbers. He brought them out of a dire strait by sheer skill, by that heartless grip of discipline which a true general exercises over his troops even at that critical moment when a common death seems to reduce all lives to an equal value.

But in the thick of it the Goorkhas - keen little Highlanders of the Indian army - looked in vain for the fighting light in their leader's eyes. They listened in vain for the encouraging voice - now low and steady in warning, now trumpet-like and maddening with the infection of excitement.

In the midst of that wild, apparently disorderly *mêlée* in the narrow valley, while the hush of mountain sunset settled over the battle, the leader sat imperturbable, cold, and infinitely wise. He was pale, and his lips were quite colourless, but his eyes were vigilant, ready, resourceful. An ideal general but no soldier. He played this game with a skill that never faced the possibility of failure - and won.

Far overhead, many miles to the northward, a solitary wanderer heard the sound of firing and paused to listen. He was a big man, worthy to be accounted such even among the strapping mountaineers of that district, and as he leant on the long barrel of his quaintly ornamental rifle his sheepskin cloak fell back from a long sinewy arm of deep-brown hue.

As he listened to the far-off rumble of independent firing he muttered to himself indications of anxiety. Strange to say, the eyes that looked out over the hollow of the gorge-like valley were blue. They were, however, hardly visible through the tangle of unkempt hair and raw wool that fell over his forehead. The high sheepskin cap was dragged forward, and the lower part of his face was almost hidden by the indiscriminate folds of hood, cloak, and scarf affected by the shepherds hereabout.

James Agar was perfectly happy. There must have been somewhere in his sporting soul that love of Nature which drives men into solitude - making game-keepers and fishermen and explorers of them. It was in this man's character to wait passive until responsibility came to him, when he accepted it readily enough; but he never went out to meet it. He was not as the sons of Levi, who took too much upon themselves; but rather was he happiest when he had only his own life and his own self to take care of.

Here he was now an outcast, an Ishmaelite, with every man's hand raised against him. It was not the first time. For this quiet-going man had unobtrusively learnt many tongues, and, while no one heeded him, he had studied the ways of this Eastern land with no mean success.

He waited there during an hour while the firing still continued, and then, when at last silence reigned again and the wind whispered undisturbed through the dark pines, he turned his wandering footsteps northward to a land where few white men have passed.

So night fell upon these two men thus hazardously brought together, and every moment stretched longer the distance between them - James Agar going north, Seymour Michael passing southward.

Agar wondered vaguely whether his toilsome diary would ever reach home, but he was not anxious as to the result of the fight which had evidently taken place in the valley. He too seemed to share the belief of all who came in contact with him that General Michael could not do wrong in warfare.

That night the Master of Stagholme laid him down to rest in the shadow of a big rock, strong in himself, strong in his faith. And as he slumbered, those who slumber not nor cease their toil by day or night sat with crooked backs over a little ticking, spitting, restless machine that spelt out his name across half the world. While the moon rose over the mountains, and looked placidly down upon this strange man lying there peacefully sleeping in a world of his own, two men who had never seen each other talked together with nimble fingers over a thousand miles of wire. And one told the other that James Edward Makerstone was dead.

The sleeper slept on. He smiled quietly beneath the moon. Perhaps he dreamt of the home-coming, of that time when he could say at last, "I have fought my fight, and now I come with a clear conscience to enjoy the good things given to me." He never dreamt of treason. He never knew that for their own gain men will sacrifice the happiness of their neighbours without so much as a pang of self-reproach. There are some people, thank Heaven, who never learn these things, who go on believing that men are good and women better all their lives.

CHAPTER XI

A CARPET KNIGHT

As children gathering pebbles on the shore.

First door on the right after passing into New Court, Trinity College, Cambridge, by the river door. It is a small door, leading directly on to a narrow, winding stone staircase. For some reason, known possibly to the architect responsible for New Court (may his bones know no rest!), the ground-floor rooms have a door of their own within the archway.

On the first floor Arthur Agar, to use the affected phraseology of an affected generation, "kept" in the days with which we have to deal. What he kept transpireth not. There were many things which he did not keep, the first among these being his money. In these rooms he dispensed an open-handed, carefully considered hospitality which earned for him a certain bubble popularity.

There are, one finds, always plenty of men (and women too) ready to lick the blacking off one's boots provided always that that doubtful fare be varied by champagne or truffles at appropriate intervals. Men came to Arthur Agar's rooms, and brought their friends. Mark well the last item. They brought their friends. There is more in that than meets the eye. There is a subtle difference between the invitation for "Mr. Jones" and the invitation for "Mr. Jones and friends" - a difference which he who runs the social race may read. If Jones is worth his salt he will discern the difference in a week.

"Oh, come to Agar's," one man (save the mark) would say to another." Ripping coffee, topping cigarettes."

So they went; they drank the ripping coffee, smoked the topping cigarette, and if they happened to be men of stomach ventured on a clinking cigar. Moreover, they were made welcome. Agar was like a vain woman who loved to see a full saloon. And he paid for his pleasure in more honourable coin than many a vain woman has laid down since daughters of Eve commenced drawing fops around them - namely, the adjectived items of hospitality above mentioned.

It did not matter much who the guests were, provided that they filled the diminutive room in those spaces left vacant by *bric-a-brac* and furniture of the spindle-legged description. So the men came. There were freshmen who fell over the footstools and bumped their heads against the painted sabots on the wall containing ever-fresh flowers, as per florist's bill; who were rather over-powered by the profusion of painted photograph frames, fans, and fal-lals. There was the man who sang a comic song and dined out on it at least twice a week. There was the calculating son of a poor North-country parson, who liked coffee after dinner and knew the value of sixpence. There was the man who came to play his own valse, and he who came to hear his own voice, *und so weiter*. Do we not know them all? Have we not run against them in after-life, despite many attempts to pass by on the other side? The habitual acceptors of hospitality have no objection to crossing the road through the thickest mud.

"By their rooms ye shall know them," might well, if profanely, be written large over any college gate. Arthur Agar's rooms were worthy of the man. There was, even on the little stone staircase, a faint odour of pastille or scent spray, or something of feminine suggestion. The unwary visitor would as likely as not catch some part of his person against a silk hanging or a lurking *portière* on crossing the threshold; and the impression which struck (as all rooms do strike) from the threshold was one of oppressive drapery. A man, by the way, should never know anything about drapery or draping. Such knowledge undermines his virility. This is an age of undermining knowledge. We all, from the lowest to the highest, learn many things of which we were better ignorant. The school-board infant acquires French; Arthur Agar and his like bring away from Cambridge a pretty knack of draping chair-backs.

There were little screens in the room, with shelves specially constructed to hold little gimcracks, which in their turn were specially shaped to stand upon the little shelves. There was a portentous standing-lamp, six feet high in its bare feet, with a shade like a crinoline. There were settees and *poufs* and *des prie-Dieu*, and strange things hanging on the wall without rhyme, reason, or beauty. And nowhere a pipe, or a tennis racket, or even a pair of boots - not so much as a single manly indiscretion in the way of a cricket-bat in the corner, or a sporting novel on the table.

In the midst of this the temporary proprietor of the rooms sat disconsolately at an inlaid writing-table with his face buried in his arms - weeping.

The outer door was shut. Arthur Agar had sported his rare oak, not to work but to weep. It sometimes does happen to men, this shedding of the idle tear, even to Englishmen, even to Cambridge men. Moreover, it was infinitely to the credit of Arthur Agar that he should bury his face in the sleeve of his perfectly-fitting coat thus and sob, for he was weeping (quietly and to himself) the advent of three thousand pounds per annum.

At his elbow lay a telegram - that flimsy pink paper which, with all our progress, all our knowledge, the bravest of us fear still.

"Jem killed in India; come home at once. - AGAR."

Honour to whom honour. Arthur Agar's only thought had been one of sudden horror. He had read the telegram over twice before going out to close his outer door. Then he came back and sat weakly down at the table where he had written more scented notes than noted themes, deliberately, womanlike, to cry.

To his credit be it noted that he never thought of Stagholme, which was now his. He only thought of Jem - his no longer - Jem the open-handed, elder brother who tolerated much and said little. Having had everything that he wanted since childhood, Arthur Agar had never been in the habit of thinking about money matters. His florist's bills (and Cambridge horticulturists seem to water their flowers with Château Lafitte), his confectioner's account, and his tailor's little note had always been paid without a murmur. Thus, want of money - the chief incentive to crime and criminal thought - had never come within measurable distance of this gentle undergraduate.

Truth to tell, he had never devoted much thought to the future. He had always vaguely concluded that his mother and Jem would "do something"; and in the meantime there were important matters requiring his attention. There was the *menu* to prepare for an approaching little dinner. There was always an approaching dinner, and always a *menu* in execrable French on a satin-faced card with the college arms in a coat of many colours. There was the florist to be interviewed and the arrangement of the table to be superintended; the finishing touch to be given to the floral decoration thereof by the master-hand.

Jem's death seemed to knock away one of the supports of the future, and Arthur Agar even in his grief was conscious of the impending necessity of having to act for himself some day.

At length he lifted his head, and through the intricate pattern of the very newest design in art muslins the daylight fell on his face. It was a face which in France is called *chiffonné*; but the term is never applied to the visage masculine. A diminutive and slightly *retrousse* nose, gentle grey eyes of the drowning-fly description, and a sensitive mouth scarcely hidden by a fair moustache of downward tendency.

Here was a man made to be ruled all his life - probably by a woman. With a little more strength it might have been a melancholy face; as it stood, it was suggestive of nothing stronger than fretfulness. There was a vague distress in the eyes and in the whole countenance which mistaken and practical souls would probably put down to a defective digestion or a feeble vitality. More than one enthusiastic disciple of Aesculapius studying at Caius professed to have discovered the evidence of some internal disease in Arthur Agar's distressed eyes; but his complaint was not of the body at all.

Presently the necessity for action forced itself upon his understanding, and he rose with a jerk. It is worth noting that his first thought was connected with dress. He passed into the inner room and there exchanged his elegant morning suit for a black one, replacing a delicate heliotrope necktie by another of sombre hue. He mentally reviewed his mourning wardrobe while doing so, and gathered much spiritual repose from the diversion.

In the meantime the Rector of Stagholme, having breakfasted, proceeded to light a cigarette and open the *Times* with the leisurely sense of enjoyment of one who takes an interest in all things without being keenly concerned in any.

"God help us!" he exclaimed suddenly; and Mrs. Glynde, who alone happened to be present, dropped a handful of housekeeping money on the floor.

"What is it, dear?" she gasped.

"There," was the answer; "read that. 'Disaster in Northern India.' Not there - higher up!"

In her eagerness Mrs. Glynde had plunged headlong into the consumption of Wesleyan missionaries in the Sandwich Islands. Then she had to find her glasses, and considerable delay was incurred by putting them on upside down. All this while the Rector sat glaring at her as if in some occult way she were responsible for the disaster in Northern India.

At last she read the short article, and was about to give a sigh of relief when her eyes travelled to a diminutive list of names appended.

"What!" she exclaimed. "What! Jem! Oh, Tom, dear, this can't be true!"

"I have no reason," answered the Rector grimly, "to suppose that it is untrue."

Mrs. Glynde was one of those unfortunate persons who seem only to have the power of aggravating at a crisis. In their way they are useful as serving to divert the mind; but they usually come in for more than their need of abuse.

The poor little woman laid the newspaper gently down by her husband's elbow, and looked at him with a certain air of grandeur and strength. The instinct that arouses the mother wren to peck at the schoolboy's hand at her nest was strong in this subdued little old lady.

"Something," she said, "must be done. How are we going to tell Dora?"

The Rector was a man who never went straight at the fence, before him. He invariably pulled up and rode alongside the obstacle before leaping, and when going for it he braced himself mentally with the reflection that he was an English gentleman, and as such had obligations. But these obligations, like those of many English gentlemen, ceased at his own fireside. He, like many of us, was apt to forget that wife, sister, and daughter are nevertheless ladies to whom deference is due.

"Oh - Dora," he answered; "she will have to bear it like the rest of us. But here am I with fresh legal complications laid upon me. I foresee endless trouble with the lawyers and that woman. Why the Squire made me his executor I can't tell. Parsons know nothing of these matters."

With a patient sigh Mrs. Glynde turned away and went to the window, where she stood with her back to him. Even to the duller masculine mind the wonder sometimes presents itself that our women-folk take us so patiently as we are. If Mrs. Glynde had turned upon her husband (who was not so selfish as he would appear), presenting him forthwith in the plainest language at her command with a piece of her mind, the treatment would have been surprising at first, and infinitely beneficial afterwards.

The Reverend Thomas sat staring into the fire - a luxury which he allowed himself all through the year - with troubled eyes. There was a fence in front of him, but he could not bring himself up to it. In his mistaken contempt for women he had never taken his wife fully into his confidence in those things - great or small, according to the capacity of the producing machine - which are essentially a personal property - namely his thoughts.

All else he told her openly and at once, as behoved an English gentleman.

Should he tell all that he had hoped and thought and

rethought respecting Jem Agar and Dora? Should he; should he not? And the loving little woman stood there almost daring to break the great silence herself; but not quite. Strong as was her mother's heart, the habit of submission was stronger. She longed, she yearned to hear the deeper, graver tone of voice which had been used once or twice towards her - once or twice in moments of unusual confidence. The Reverend Thomas Glynde was silent, and the voice that they both heard was Dora's, singing as she came downstairs towards them. It was only a matter of moments, and when we have no more than that wherein to act we usually take the wrong turning.

Mrs. Glynde turned and gave one imploring look towards her husband.

At the same instant the door opened and Dora entered, singing as she came.

"What is the matter?" she exclaimed. "You both look depressed. Stocks down, or something else has gone up? I know! Papa has been made a bishop!"

With a cheery laugh she went to the table and took up the newspaper.

CHAPTER XII

BAD NEWS

Sa manière de souffrir est le témoignage qu'une âme porte sur elle-même.

There was a horrid throbbing silence while Dora read, and her parents calculated the seconds which would necessarily elapse before she reached the bottom line. Such moments as these are scored up as years in the span of life.

Mrs. Glynde did not know what she was doing. It happened that she was trying to rub away a flaw in the window-glass with her pocket hand-kerchief - a flaw which must have been an old friend, as such things are in quiet lives. At this occupation she found herself when her heart began to beat again.

"I suppose," said Dora in a terribly calm voice, "that the *Times* never makes a mistake - I mean they never publish anything unless they are quite sure?"

Then the English gentleman of parts who ever and anon peeped out through the veneer of the parson asserted himself - the English gentleman whose sense of fair play and honour told him that it is better to strike at once a blow that must be struck than to keep

Henry Seton Merriman

the victim waiting.

"Such is their reputation," answered Dora's father.

Mrs. Glynde turned with that pathetic yearning movement of a punished dog which waits to be called. But Dora had some of her father's sternness, her father's good British reserve, and she never called.

Turning, she walked quietly out of the room. And all the light had gone out of her life. So we write, and so ye read; but do we realise it? It is not many of us who have suddenly to look at life without so much as a glimmer in its dark recesses to make it worth the living. It is not many of us who come to be told by the doctor: "For the rest of your existence you must give up eyesight," or, "For the remainder of life you must go halt." But these are trifles. Everything is a trifle, if we would only believe it. Riches and poverty, peace and war, fame and obscurity, town and country, England and the backwoods - all these are trifles compared with that other life which makes our own a living completeness.

Silently she went, and left silence behind her. The Rector was abashed. For once a woman had acted in a manner unexpected by him; for he was ignorant enough of the world to keep up the old fallacy of treating women as a class. True, it was Dora, whom he held apart from the rest of her sex; but still he was left wondering. He felt as if he had been found walking in a holy place with shoes upon his feet - those gross shoes of Self with which most of us tramp through the world, not heeding where we tread or what we crush.

One of the hardest things we have to bear is the

helpless standing by while one dear to us must suffer. When Mrs. Glynde turned round and came towards her husband she had become an old woman. Her face had suddenly aged while her frame was yet in its full strength, and such a change is not pleasant to look on.

"Tom," she said, in a dry, commanding voice, "you must go up to the Holme at once and hear what news they have. There may be some chance - it may please God to spare us yet."

"Yes," answered the Rector meekly; "I will go."

While he was lacing his boots with all speed Mrs. Glynde took up the newspaper again, and reread the brief account of the disaster. They were spared comment; that blow came later, when the warriors of Fleet Street set about explaining why the defeat was sustained and why it should never have happened. In due course these carpet tacticians proved to their own satisfaction that Colonel Stevenor was incompetent for the service on which he had been dispatched. But the reek of printing-ink never was good for the better feelings.

In due course the Rector set off across the park; very grave, and distinctly aware of the importance of his mission. He had somewhere in his composition a strong sense of the dramatic, to which the situation appealed. He felt that had he been a younger man he would have stored up many details during the morning's work worthy of reproduction in the narrative form during years to come.

Before he reached the great house he was aware that the grim pleasure of imparting bad news was not to be his, for the blinds were all lowered - a detail likely to receive early attention in a feminine household, for it is only men who can hear of a death without thinking of mourning and the blinds.

The butler opened the door and took the Rector's hat and stick with a silent *savoir-faire* indicative of experience in well-bred grief. His chaste demeanour said as plainly as words that this was right and proper, the Rector being no more than he expected.

"Where's your mistress?" asked Mr. Glynde, who had strong views upon butlers in general and Tims in particular - said Tims being so sure of his place that he did not always trouble to know it.

"Library, sir," replied Tims in an appropriately sepulchral voice.

The Rector went to the library without waiting to be announced. He was a man well versed in human nature, as most parsons are, and it is possible that he had caught a glimpse of Mrs. Agar watching his advent from the dining-room window.

The lady of the house was standing by the writing-table when he entered, and beneath her ill-concealed excitement there was something subtly observant, like the glance of an untruthful child, which he never forgot nor forgave, despite his cloth and the impossibilities popularly expected therefrom.

"Oh," she exclaimed, "it is you. I have telegraphed for Arthur. I have - telegraphed for Arthur."

"Why?"

She gave a nervous, almost a guilty little laugh, and looked at him with puzzled discomfort.

"Why?" he repeated, looking at her with a cold scrutiny much dreaded of the parish ne'er-do-wells.

"Oh, well," she replied, "it is only natural that I should want him at home in such a time as this - such a terrible affliction. Besides -"

"Besides," suggested the Rector imperturbably, "he is now master of Stagholme."

"Yes!" she said, with a simulated surprise which would scarcely have deceived the most guileless Sunday-school teacher. "I had not thought of that. I suppose something must be done at once - those horrid lawyers again."

Her eyes were dancing with breathless excitement. To this woman excitement even in the form of a death was better than nothing. The bourgeois mind, with its love of a Crystal Palace, a subscription dance, or even a parochial bazaar, was unquenchable even after years of practice as the county lady of position.

The Rector did not answer. He stood squarely in front of her with a persistence that forced her to turn shiftily away with a pretence of looking at the clock.

"This is a bad business," he said. "That boy ought never to have gone out there."

Mrs. Agar had her handkerchief ready and made use of it, with as much effect upon Mr. Glynde as might have been produced upon a granite sphinx. There is no man harder to deceive than the innately good and conscientious man of the world who has tried to find good in human nature.

"Poor boy!" sobbed the lady. "Dear Jem! I could not keep him at home." Thus proving herself a fool, and worse, before those wise eyes.

When occasion demanded Mr. Glynde could wield a very strong silence - stronger than he thought. He wielded it now, and Mrs. Agar shuffled before it, her eyes glittering with suppressed communicativeness. She was obviously bubbling over with talk relevant and irrelevant, but the Rector had the chivalry to check it by his cold silence.

After a pause it was he who spoke, in a quiet, unemotional voice which aggravated while it cowed her.

"When did you hear this news?" he asked.

"Oh, last night. It was so late that I did not send down. I - it was so sudden. I was terribly upset."

"M - yes."

"I telegraphed to Arthur first thing this morning," the mistress of Stagholme went on eagerly, "and I was just going to write to you when you came in."

With that nervous desire for corroborative evidence which arouses the suspicion of the observant whenever it appears, Mrs. Agar indicated the writing-table with open blotter and inkstand. Instantly, but too late, she regretted having done so, for a volume playfully called

"Every Man his own Lawyer" lay confessed beside the writing-case, and its home on the bookshelf stared vacantly at them.

"And from whom did you hear it?" pursued the Rector, heartlessly looking at the book with an air of recognition.

"Oh, from a Mr. Johnson - at the War Office, or the India Office, or somewhere. I suppose I ought to write and thank him. Let me see - where is the telegram?"

She shuffled among the papers on the writing-table, and made the hideous mistake of pushing "Every Man his own Lawyer" behind the stationery case.

"Here it is!" she exclaimed at length.

It was a long document. Mr. Johnson, not having to pay for telegraphic expenses out of his own pocket, had done his task thoroughly. He stated clearly that the advance column under Colonel Stevenor, Major Agar, and another British officer had been surprised and annihilated. There were no particulars yet, nor could reliable details be expected, as it was quite certain that not one man of the ill-fated corps had survived. General Seymour, added the official, missing out in his haste the commanding officer's surname, had promptly repaired to the scene of the disaster, to punish the victors, and, if possible, recover the effects of the slain.

Mrs. Agar was one of those persons who are incapable of reading a letter or a telegram thoroughly. She was one of those for whose comprehension the wrong end of the story must have been specially created. Had the official put Seymour Michael's name in full, it is probable that in her infantile excitement she would have failed to take it in or to connect it with the man who had wronged her twenty years before.

She had not thought much about that little affair during late years, her feeling for Seymour Michael having settled down into a passive hatred. The longing to do him some personal injury had died away fifteen years before. She was, as a matter of fact, quite incapable of a lasting feeling of any description. Hers was a life lived for the present only. A tea-party next week was of more importance to her than a change in fortune next year. Some people are thus, and Heaven help those whose lives come under their fickle influence!

The one permanent motive of her existence was her son Arthur - the puny little infant who had been prematurely ushered into a world that seemed full of hatred twenty years before - and even his image faded from mind and thought before the short Cambridge terms were half expired.

At this moment she was thinking less of the death of Jem than of the approaching arrival of Arthur. There must have been something wrong with her mental focus, to which trifles presented themselves as of the first importance, to the obliteration of larger matters.

"And this is all the news you have had?" inquired the Rector, rather hurriedly. He saw Sister Cecilia coming up the avenue, and that lady was for him the embodiment of the combination of those feminine failings which aggravated him so intensely.

"Yes."

He moved towards the door, and standing there he turned, holding up a warning finger.

"You must be very careful," he said. "You must not consult any lawyer or take any steps in this matter. So far as you are concerned the state of affairs is unchanged. I, as the Squire's executor, am the only person called upon to act in any way if that poor boy has died without making a will. You must remember that your son is under age."

With that he left her, rather precipitately, for Sister Cecilia, like all busybodies, was a quick walker.

In a few moments Miss Cecilia Harbottle entered the library. She glided forward as if afloat on a depth of the milk of human kindness, and folded Mrs. Agar in an emotional embrace.

"Dear!" she exclaimed. "Dear Anna, how I feel for you!"

In illustration of this sympathy she patted Mrs. Agar's somewhat flabby hands, and looked softly at her. She could hardly have failed to see a glitter in the bereaved one's eyes, which was certainly not that of grief. It was the gleam of pure, heartless excitement and love of change. But Sister Cecilia probably misread it; for, like all excesses, that of charity seems to dull the comprehension.

"Tell me, dear," she urged gently, "all about it."

How many of us imagine the satisfaction of our own curiosity to be sympathy!

So Mrs. Agar told her all about it, and presently they sat down, with a view to fuller discussion. There was, however, a point beyond which even Mrs. Agar would not go. This point Sister Cecilia scented with the instinct of the terrier, so keen was her nose in the sniffing of other people's business. When that point was reached a third time she gently led the way over it.

"Of course," she said, with a resigned glance at the curtain poles, "one cannot help sometimes feeling that a wise Providence does all for the best."

Gratifying as this must have been to the power in question, no miraculous manifestation of joy was forthcoming, and Mrs. Agar cunningly confined herself to a non-committing "Yes."

After a sigh, Sister Cecilia further expatiated.

"I cannot but think," she said, "that Stagholme will be in better hands now. Of course dear Jem was very nice, and all that - a dear, good boy. But do you not think that Arthur is more suited to the position in some ways?"

"Perhaps he is," allowed Mrs. Agar, with ill-concealed pleasure.

"He is," continued Sister Cecilia, with a broader brush, "so refined, so gentlemanly, so ideal a country squire."

And after that she had no difficulty in supplying herself with information.

CHAPTER XIII

ON THIN ICE

Treason doth never prosper. What's the reason?
For if it prosper, none dare call it treason.

Two days later a gentleman, whose clean-shaven face
had a habit of beaming suddenly into a professional
smile, was seated at a huge writing-table in his office
in Gray's Inn, when a clerk announced to him the
arrival of Mrs. Agar, who desired to see him at once.

Mr. Rigg beamed instantaneously, and the clerk, who
knew his master, waited until the paroxysm had
passed. In the meantime Mrs. Agar was fuming in the
waiting-room, wherein lay a copy of the *Times* and
nothing else. The window looked out upon the neatly
kept but depressing garden, where five antiquated
rooks looked in vain for sustenance. Mrs. Agar
watched these intelligent birds, but all her soul was in
her ears. She had already set Mr. Rigg down in her
own mind as a stupid because, forsooth, he had dared
to keep her waiting.

But the truth is that they are accustomed to ladies in
Gray's Inn, especially ladies in deep mourning, with a
chastely important air which seems to demand that
advice and sympathy be carefully mingled. *Connues,*

these ladies whose deep crape and quite exceptional bereavement plead (not always dumbly) for a special equity, home-made and superior to any law, and infer that the ordinary foes are in their case more than any gentleman would think of accepting.

The clerk presently passed into an inner room and fetched therefrom a tin box, upon which were painted in dingy white the letters "J. E. M. A.," and underneath "Stagholme Estate." This the embryo lawyer carefully wiped with a duster, and set it up on some of its fellows immediately behind Mr. Rigg.

There was no hurry displayed in this scenic arrangement. Mr. Rigg made a practice of keeping ladies, especially those wearing crape, for a few minutes in the waiting-room. It calmed them down wonderfully, and introduced into their mental chambers a little legal atmosphere.

"Marks," he said, when that youth was taking his last look round at the *mise en scène* before, as it were, raising the curtain, "eh - er - just go round to Corbyn's and get them to make up these pills."

At the mention of the medicinal term he beamed, as if to intimate that between themselves no secret need be observed that he, Mr. Rigg, was subject to the usual anatomical laws of mankind.

"And - er - just call at the fishmonger's as you come back and get a parcel for me, ordered this morning."

"Yes, sir," answered the faithful Marks, taking the prescription as if it were a will or a transfer.

He knew his part so well that he moved towards the door and opened it as if Mrs. Agar's existence and attendance in the waiting-room were matters of the utmost indifference.

"Marks!"

The door was open, so that the lawyer's voice carried well down the passage.

"Yes, sir."

"I will see Mrs. Agar now."

And Mrs. Agar was shown in, all bustling with excitement.

"Mr. Rigg," she said, with some dignity, "has Mr. Glynde been here?"

The lawyer beamed again - literally all over his parchment-coloured face, except the eyes, which remained grave.

"When, my dear madam?" he asked, as he brought forward a chair.

"Well, lately - since my son's death."

The lawyer opened a large diary, and proceeded to trace back each day with his finger. It promised to be a question of time, this ascertaining whether Mr. Glynde had called within the last week. It was marvellous how well this man of deeds knew his clients. Mrs. Agar had never persevered in any inquiry or project that required time all through her life. Mr. Rigg, behind his disarming smile, could see as far into a crape veil as any man.

"It must have been quite lately," said Mrs. Agar, leaning forward and trying visibly to read the diary.

Mr. Rigg turned back a few pages, as if to go over the ground a second time.

"Let me see!" he said leisurely. "What was the precise date of the - er - sad event?"

"Last Tuesday, the fourteenth."

"To be sure," reflected Mr. Rigg, fixing his eyes sadly on an engraving of London Bridge in the seventeenth century - a spot specially reserved for the sadder moments of probate and other testamentary work. "Very sad, very sad."

Then he rose with the mental brushing-away of unshed tears of a man who has never yet had time in life for idle lamentation. He turned towards the tin box, jingling his keys in a most practical and business-like way.

"And I presume," he said, "that you have come to consult me about the late Captain Agar's will?"

"Was there a will?" asked Mrs. Agar, with audible alarm. She had not studied "Every Man his own Lawyer" quite in vain, although most of the legal technicalities had conveyed nothing whatever to her mind. She did not notice that her question regarding Mr. Glynde had never been answered.

Mr. Rigg turned upon her beaming.

"I have no will," he answered. "I thought that perhaps you were aware of the existence of one."

Mrs. Agar's face lighted up.

"No," she said, with ill-concealed delight; "I am certain there is no will."

"Indeed! And why, my dear madam?"

"Well - oh, well, because Jem was just the sort of person to forget such matters. Besides, when he left England he was under age."

The lawyer was looking at her with his usual sympathetic smile spread over his face like an actor's make-up, but his eyes were very keen and clever.

"Of course," he observed, "he may have made one out there."

"I do not think that it is likely," replied the lady, whose small thoughts always came into the world in charge of a very obvious father in the shape of a wish. "There are no facilities out there - no lawyers."

"There are quite a number of lawyers in India," said Mr. Rigg, with sudden gravity. His face was only grave when he wished to fend off laughter.

"Well," persisted Mrs. Agar, "I am *sure* Jem did not make a will."

Mr. Rigg bowed and resumed his seat. He took up a

penholder and smiled, presumably at his own sunny thoughts.

Mrs. Agar was one of those fatuous ladies who think themselves capable of tricking a professional man out of his fee. She had a vague notion that if one asks a lawyer a question the price of his answer is at least six shillings and eightpence. Up to this point in the interview she was serenely conscious of having eluded the fee.

"I presume," she remarked carelessly, in pursuance of this economical policy, "that in such a case the property would go unconditionally to the second son."

"There are contingent possibilities," replied the man of subterfuge blandly. He did not mean anything at all, but shrewdly guessed that Mrs. Agar would not credit him with so simple a design.

The lady smiled in a subtly commiserating manner, indicative of the fact that on some family matters the ignorance of all except herself was somewhat pitiful.

"Of course," she said, "as regards the present case, I know perfectly well that both Jem and his father would wish everything to go to Arthur."

She was picking a thread from the corner of her jacket with an air of nonchalance.

Mr. Rigg was silent. He had some thirty years before this period given up attaching importance to the wishes of the deceased as interpreted by disinterested survivors.

"And *I* should imagine that the necessary transfers - and - and things would be much better put in hand at once. Delay seems to me quite unnecessary."

She paused for Mr. Rigg's opinion - quite a friendly opinion, of course, without price.

"Pardon me," said that lawyer, driven into a corner at last, "but are you consulting me on behalf of the late Squire's executor, Mr. Glynde, or on your own account?"

"Oh!" replied Mrs. Agar, drawing herself up with a deprecating little laugh, "I did not intend it to be a consultation at all. I happened to be passing, that was all. You see, Mr. Rigg, Mr. Glynde does not know anything about these matters. Clergymen are so stupid."

"Seems to be afraid," Mr. Rigg was reflecting behind his pleasant mask, "of the young man coming alive again."

Mrs. Agar was like a child in many ways, more especially in her unbounded belief in her own cunning. She actually imagined herself to be a match for this man, who had been trained in the ways of duplicity all his life. She saw nothing of his mind, and fatuously ignored the fact that from the moment she had entered the room he had begun the interview with a mental hypothesis.

"This woman," he had reflected, "has always hated her step-son. She got him a commission in an Indian regiment for the primary purpose of getting him out of the way while she saved money on her life-interest in the estate for her second son. The secondary purpose was little more than a hope. She hoped for the best. The best has come off, and she is not clever enough to let things take their course."

Every word Mrs. Agar had uttered, every silence, every glance had gone to confirm the lawyer's opinion, and he sat pleasantly beaming on her. He did not jump up and denounce her, for lawyers are scientists. As a doctor in the pursuit of his science does not hesitate to handle foul things, to probe horrid sores, so the lawyer must needs smirch his hands even to the elbow in those moral tumours from whence emanate the thousand and one domestic crimes which will ever remain just outside the pale of the law. And in one as in the other the finer susceptibilities grow dull. The doctor almost forgets the pain he inflicts. The lawyer gradually loses his sense of right and wrong.

Mr. Rigg was an honest man - as honesty is understood in the law. He was keenly alive to all the motives of this woman, who, in the law of humanity, was a criminal. He had started from a lawyer's standpoint - *id est*, personal advantage. "To whose advantage?" they ask, and there they assign the action. But Mr. Rigg was also a good lawyer, and therefore he kept his own counsel.

"Things must be allowed," he said, "to take their course. You know, Mrs. Agar, we are proverbially slow in moving, but we are sure."

Now it happened that this was precisely the position assumed by Mr. Glynde, whose respect for legal routine was enormous. He rarely moved in any matters wherein the law could by hook or crook be introduced without consulting Mr. Rigg, whom he vaguely called his "man." And it was precisely this delay that Mrs. Agar disliked. She had no definite reason for so doing; but this stroke of good fortune presented itself to her mind more in the light of an opportunity to be seized than as a just inheritance to be thankfully received in its due time.

She was awake to the fact that Arthur was not the man to seize any opportunity, however obviously it might be thrust into his grasp, and her knowledge of the world tended to exaggerate its dishonesty in her mind.

Sister Cecilia and she had talked this matter over with that small modicum of learning which is a dangerous thing, and they had arrived at the conclusion that Mr. Glynde was not competent to carry out the duties thus suddenly thrust upon him. Wrapped up as was her heart in the welfare of her weakling son, the one lasting motive of her life had been to secure for him the largest possible portion of earthly goods. Now that success seemed to be within measurable distance, she gave way to the baneful panic of the weak conspirator, and fancied that the whole world was allied against her.

She could not keep her fingers off "Every Man his own Lawyer," and consulted that boon to the legal profession to such good effect that she placed a handsome fee in the pocket of one of its brightest ornaments at the earliest opportunity. Mr. Rigg continued to beam and to keep his own counsel, merely notifying that things must be allowed to take their own course, and presently he bowed Mrs. Agar out of his office, dissatisfied, and with an uncomfor-table feeling of having been somewhat indiscreet.

Arthur was waiting for her in a hansom cab in Holborn, and with a sigh of relief they drove westward to a shop in Regent Street to order a supply of the newest procurable mode of signifying grief on paper and envelopes. Arthur Agar was an expert in such matters, and indeed both mother and son were more at home in the graceful pastime of spending money than in the technicalities of making or keeping the same.

Arthur was already beginning to taste the sweetness of his adversity, and being intensely sensitive to the influence of those with whom he happened to be at the moment, he was already beginning to look back with mild surprise to the first burst of grief to which he had given way on hearing that Jem was killed.

CHAPTER XIV

THE CURSE OF A GOOD INTENTION

There is one that keepeth silence and is found wise.

Sister Cecilia received - nay, she almost welcomed - the news of Jem Agar's death in an intensely Christian spirit. She looked upon it in the light of a chastening-a sort of moral cold bath, unpleasant at the time, but cleanly and refreshing in its effect. Intense goodness and virtue of the jubby-jubby order seem frequently to produce this result. Trouble - provided that it be not personal - is elevated to a position which it was never intended to occupy by an all-seeing Providence. There are some people who step into the troubles of others as into the chastening bath above referred to, and splash about. They pretend to feel deeply bereavements which cannot reasonably be expected to affect them, and go about the world with a well-scrubbed air of conscious virtue, saying in manner if not in words, "Look at me; my troubles compass me about, but my innate good-ness enables me to take them in the proper spirit and to be cheerful despite all."

This was precisely Sister Cecilia's attitude towards her small world of Stagholme, after the news of the young Squire's death had cast a gloom over the whole neighbourhood.

Henry Seton Merriman

"Ah!" she would say to some honest cottage mother who had more true feeling in her rough little finger than Sister Cecilia possessed in her whole heart. "These trials are sent to us for our good. The ways of Providence are strange, Mrs. Martin - strange to us now."

"Yes, miss; that they be," Mrs. Martin replied, looking at her with the hard and far-seeing gaze of a poor mother who has known trouble in its least romantic form. And Sister Cecilia, with that blindness which comes from systematically closing the eyes to the earthly side of earthly things, never realised that the small change of sympathy is often slightly aggravating.

At this period she took to calling Jem Agar her "poor boy." The grave seems to have the power of completely altering the past, and with persons of the stamp of Sister Cecilia death appears not only to wipe out all sin, but to impair the memory of the living to such an extent that the individuality of the deceased is no longer recognisable.

Jem never had in any sense of the word been her boy. His feelings for her had passed from the distrust of childhood to the lofty contempt of a schoolboy for all things preternaturally virtuous, finally settling down into the more tolerant contempt of manhood. The dead, however, have perforce to accept much affection which they scornfully refused in life.

"Poor Jem!" said Sister Cecilia to Mrs. Agar the day after that lady's visit to Gray's Inn. "I always thought that perhaps he and dear Dora would come to - to some understanding."

She stirred her tea with patient, suffering head inclined at a resigned angle.

"Do you think there *was* any understanding between them?" inquired Mrs. Agar.

"Well - I should not like to say."

Which, being translated, meant that she would like to say, but did not know.

It had always been a pet scheme of Mrs. Agar's that Dora should marry Arthur; firstly, because she would have nearly two thousand pounds a year on the death of her parents; and, secondly, because she was a capable person with plenty of common-sense. These two adjuncts - namely, money and common-sense - Mrs. Agar wisely looked for in candidates for the flaccid hand of her son.

"I will try and find out," said Sister Cecilia after a pause.

Mrs. Agar said nothing. She was meditating over this last stroke of fate in favour of her scheme, and her thoughts were disturbed by that distrust in the continuance of good fortune which usually spoils the enjoyment of the unscrupulous in those good things which they have obtained for themselves.

So Sister Cecilia took it for granted that she was doing the will of the mistress of Stagholme when she wrote a note that same evening inviting Dora to have tea with her the following afternoon.

At the hour appointed Dora arrived, and was duly

shown into the little cottage drawing-room, of which the decoration hovered between the avowedly devout and the economo-aesthetic.

Sister Cecilia swept down upon her with a speechless emotion which, in the nature of things (and Sister Cecilia), could not well be of long duration.

"My dear," she whispered, "God will give you strength to bear this awful trial."

Dora recovered her breath and re-arranged her crushed habiliments before inquiring, with just sufficient feeling to save her from downright rudeness, "What is the matter; has something else happened?"

Sister Cecilia drew back. She was vaguely conscious of having run mentally against a brick wall. There was something new and unusual about Dora which she could not understand - something, if she could only have seen it, suggestive of the quiet, strong man in whose honour the whole parish wore mourning. But Sister Cecilia was not a subtle woman. She had had so little experience of the world, of men and of women, that she fell easily into the error of thinking that they were all to be treated alike and with equal success by little maxims culled from fourpenny-halfpenny devotional books.

"No, dear," she exclaimed; "I was referring to our terrible loss. My heart has been bleeding for you -"

"It is very kind, I'm sure," said Dora quietly; "I forgot that I had not seen you since the news reached us."

It is probable that her self-control cost her more than

she suspected. Her lips were drawn and dry. She wore a thick veil, which she carefully abstained from lifting above the level of her eyes. "I am sure," moaned Sister Cecilia, "it has been a most trying time for us all. I wonder that Mrs. Agar has borne up so bravely. Her health is wonderful, considering."

Dora sat looking straight in front of her. She was withdrawing her gloves slowly. Her face was that of a person whose mind was made up for the endurance of an operation.

The twaddling voice, the characteristic reference to health, were intensely aggravating. There are some women who talk of their own health before the dead are buried. They do not seem to be able to separate grief from bodily ill. Clad in crape, they rush to the seaside, and there, presumably because grief affects their legs, they hire a man to wheel themselves and Sorrow in a bath-chair. Why - oh, why! does bereavement drive women into bath-chairs on the King's Road, or the Lees, or the Hoe?

"Wonderful!" said Dora.

Sister Cecilia, busying herself with the teapot, proceeded to blow her own trumpet with the barefacedness of true virtue.

"I have been with her constantly," she said. "I think it is better for us all to tell of our grief; I think that we are given speech for that purpose. For although one may only be able to offer sympathy and perhaps a little advice, it is always a relief to speak of one's sorrow."

"I suppose it is," admitted Dora from her strong-hold

of reserve, "for some people."

"Oh, yes!" exclaimed Sister Cecilia, all heedless of the sarcasm. For extreme charity is proof against such. It covers other things besides a multitude of sins. Wielded foolishly it runs amuck like a too luxuriant creeper, and often kills commonsense. "And that is why I asked you to come, dear. I thought that you might want to confide in some one - that you might want to unburden your heart to one who feels for you as if this sorrow were her own -"

"Only one piece of sugar, thank you," interrupted Dora. "Thank you. No. Bread and butter, please. It is very kind of you, Sister Cecilia. But, you see, when I have any unburdening to do there is always mother, and if I want any advice there is always father."

"Yes, dear. But sometimes even one's parents are not quite the persons to whom one would turn in times of grief."

"Oh!" observed Dora, without much enthusiasm.

Unconsciously Sister Cecilia was doing the very best thing possible for Dora, She was arousing in her the spirit of antagonism - hardening a stricken heart, as it were, by a fresh challenge. She was teaching Dora to fight for what we learn to deem most sacred - namely, the right to monopolise our own thoughts and feelings. Sister Cecilia is not, one may assume, the only good woman in the world who cannot draw a definite line between sympathy and mere curiosity. With many the display of sympathy is nothing but a half-conscious bait to attract a shoal of further details.

Self-reliance was lurking somewhere in this girl's character, but it had never been developed by the pressure of circumstances. Reserve she had seen practised by her father, but the actual advantages thereof were only now beginning to be apparent to her. The body, we are told, adapts itself to abnormal circumstances; so is it with the mind. Already Dora was beginning, as they say at sea, to find her feet; to take that stand amidst her environments which she was forced to hold, practically alone, thereafter.

And Sister Cecilia, with that blind faith in a good motive which gives almost as much trouble as actual vice, floundered on in the path she had mapped out for herself.

"You know, dear," she said, looking out of the window with a sentimental droop of her thin, inquisitive lips, "I cannot help feeling that this - this terrible blow means more to you than it does to us."

"Why?" inquired Dora practically.

Sister Cecilia was silent, with one of those aggravating silences which do not allow even the satisfaction of a flat contradiction. A meaning silence is a coward's argument. She was beginning to feel slightly nervous before this child, ignorant that childhood is not always a matter of years and calendar months.

"Why?" asked Dora again.

Sister Cecilia looked rather bewildered.

"Well, dear, I thought perhaps - I always thought that

my poor boy entertained some feeling - you understand?"

"No," replied Dora, borrowing for the moment her father's most crushing deliberation of manner, "I cannot say I do. When you say your 'poor boy,' are you referring to Jem?"

Sister Cecilia assented with a resigned nod worthy of the very earliest martyr.

"Then, as every one has discovered so many virtues in him - quite suddenly - we had better emulate one of them, and have at the least the good feeling to hold our tongues about any feelings he may have entertained. Do you not think so, Sister Cecilia?"

"Well, dear, I only thought to act as might be best for you," said the well-intentioned meddler, with the drawl of the professionally misunderstood.

"I have no doubt of that," returned Dora, with an equanimity which was again strangely suggestive of Jem Agar. "But in future you will be consulting my welfare much more effectively by refraining from action on my behalf at all."

"As you will, dear; as you will," in the hopeless tone of age, experience, and wisdom forced to stand idle while youth and folly rush headlong down the hill.

"Yes," returned Dora calmly; "I know that, thank you. And now, I think, we had better change the subject."

The subject was therefore changed; but Sister Cecilia, having, as it were, whetted her appetite for details, was not at her ease with other food for the mind, and presently Dora left.

The girl went back into her small world with a new knowledge gained - the knowledge that in all and through all we are really quite alone. There can be only one companion, and if that one be absent, there are only so many talking-machines left to us. And many of us pass the whole of our lives in conversation with them. So it is; and we know not why.

In a subtle way she felt stronger for this little tussle - a fight is always exhilarating. She felt that from henceforth the memory of Jem was hers, and hers alone, to defend and to cherish. It was not much of a consolation. No. But then this is a world of small mercies, where some of us get an hour or some mean portion of a day when we want a lifetime.

Henry Seton Merriman

CHAPTER XV

THE TOUCH OF NATURE

A sense, when first I fronted him,
Said, "Trust him not!"

After successfully carrying through the purchase of
mourning stationery and attending to other important
items connected with sorrow in its worldly shape,
Arthur Agar went back to Cambridge. There was
enough of the woman in his nature to enable him to
cherish grief and nurse it lovingly, as some women
(not the best of them) do. In this attitude towards the
world there was none of that dogged going about his
business which characterises the ordinary man from
whose life something has slipped out.

He wandered by the banks of the Cam with mourning
in his mien, and his cherished friends took sympathetic
coffee with him after Hall. They spoke of Jem with
that fervid admiration which University men honestly
feel for one a few years their senior who has already
"done something."

"A ripping soldier" they called him and some of them
entertained serious doubts as to whether they had done
wisely in choosing the less glorious paths of peace.
And Arthur Agar settled down into the old profitless

life, with this difference - that he could not dine out, that he used blackedged notepaper, and that his delicate heliotrope neckties were folded away in a drawer until such time as his grief should be assuaged into that state of resignation technically called half-mourning.

One afternoon well towards the end of the term Arthur Agar's "gyp" crept in with that valet-like confidential air which seems to be bred of too intimate a knowledge of the extent of one's wardrobe.

"There is a gentleman, sir," he said, "as wants to see you. But in no wise will he give his name, which, he says, you don't know it."

"Is he selling engravings?" asked Arthur.

The "gyp" looked mildly offended. As if he didn't know that sort!

"No, sir. Military man, I should take it."

Arthur Agar had met the Scotch Balaclava veteran in his time too. He hesitated, and the "gyp," who felt that his reputation was at stake, spoke:

"He is eminently a gentleman, sir," he said.

"Well, then, show him up."

A moment later a man who might have been the wandering Jew *fin de siècle* stood in the doorway. His smart military moustache was small and evidently trimmed, his face was sunburnt, and in his eyes there gleamed the restlessness of India.

He bowed, and awaited the exit of the man. Then, coming forward, he was able for the first time to see Arthur Agar's face distinctly, and his glance wavered.

At that moment Arthur Agar was staring at him with something in his face that was almost strong. When this man had entered the room, Arthur felt his heart give one great bound which almost choked him. There was a strange physical feeling of vacuity in his breast which seemed to paralyse his breathing powers, and his temples throbbed painfully.

Arthur Agar's life had been passed in eminently pleasant places. The seamy side of existence had always been carefully hidden from his eyes. He therefore did not recognise this strange sense which had leapt into his being - the sense of superhuman, physical, mortal revulsion.

He was divided between two instincts. One side of his nature urged him to shriek like a woman. Had he followed the other, he would have rushed at this man, whom he had never seen before, seeking to do him bodily harm. He would not have paused to reason that in anything like a struggle he would stand no chance against the sinewy, dark-eyed soldier who stood watching him. For there are moments even in this age of self-suppression when we do not pause to think, when he who cannot swim will leap into deep water to save another.

This sudden unreasoning hatred, so foreign to his gentle nature, seemed to stagger Arthur Agar as the sudden intimation of some mortal disease lurking in his own being would have done. He gripped the back of the spindle-legged chair, and could find no word to say. The stranger it was who spoke.

"I presume," he said, with a pleasant smile, in a voice so musical that his hearer breathed suddenly as if his head had been lifted from water, "I presume that you are Mr. Arthur Agar?"

While he spoke he looked past Arthur, out of the silken-draped window. He did not seem to like the glance of this young man, for even the most practical of us have a conscience at times.

"Yes."

The new-comer laid his walking-stick on the table, and turned to make sure that the door was closed.

"I knew your step-brother," he explained, "Jem Agar, in India."

Then the instinct of the gentleman and the host asserted itself over and above the throbbing hatred.

"Ah! Will you sit down?"

The stranger took the proffered chair and laid aside his hat. But neither of them was at ease. There was a subtle suggestion that they had met before and quarrelled - vague, unreasoning, quite impossible if you will; but it was there. They were as men meeting again with a past between them (too full of strong passions ever to be forgotten) which each was trying in vain to ignore.

"I have brought home a few belongings of his," the stranger went on to explain. "Just a port-manteau with some clothes and things."

He paused, and drew a small packet from the pocket of a covert-coat which he carried over his arm.

"Here," he went on, "are some papers of his - a diary and one or two letters. The rest of the things are at my hotel in town."

Arthur took the packet, and, still in the same dreamy, unreal way, opened it. He turned to the last entry - dated six weeks back.

"Got out of bed at five, but nothing to be seen in the valley. I feel a bit chippy this morning. If nothing turns up to-day shall begin to feel uneasy. The men seem all right. They are plucky little fellows."

There was a self-consciousness about Jem Agar's diary, a selection of the right word, which conveyed nothing to Arthur. But it fell into other hands later on, where it was understood better.

General Michael was watching the undergraduate with the same critical attention which he had brought to bear on the writer of the diary not two months before.

"Did you see much of your step-brother?" he asked abruptly, feeling his way towards his purpose.

Arthur looked up. He was getting accustomed to the loathing that he felt for this man, as one gets accustomed to an evil odour or a physical pain.

"I saw enough of him to be very fond of him," he replied.

"And your mother - was she attached to him? Excuse my asking; I have a reason."

The little pause was enough. Seymour Michael had expected as much.

He had never forgiven Mrs. Agar the insults she heaped upon his head in the drawing-room of Jaggery House. It is very difficult to bring shame home to a Jew, and on that occasion this son of the modern Ishmaelites had been thoroughly ashamed of himself. The sting of that past ignominy was with him still, and would remain within his heart until such time as he could revenge himself.

With that mean, underhand watchfulness for an opportunity which is almost excusable in one of the unfortunates against whom every man's hand is raised to-day, he had never parted with his thirst for revenge. The moment seemed propitious. It was within his power to lay for Anna Agar one of those spiteful feminine traps of which a woman can only fully appreciate the sting.

He determined to leave Mrs. Agar in ignorance of the real facts respecting her step-son. His vengeance was to allow her to rejoice - almost openly, as she did - in the stroke of fortune by which her own son, Arthur, had become possessed of Stagholme. He knew the woman well enough to foresee that in a hundred ways she would heap up ignominy, meanness, deception, which would crumble in one vast wreck about her head when Jem Agar returned.

It was a vengeance worthy of the man, and spiteful enough to be fully comprehended by its victim. But, like others handling petards, Seymour Michael grew somewhat careless, and forgot that the wrong man is sometimes hoist.

He knew his position well enough to make all safe as regarded Jem Agar on his return. It was absolutely necessary to tell Arthur Agar - necessary for his own safety in the future. The other two persons to whom the secret was to be imparted were Mrs. Agar and Dora Glynde. From Mrs. Agar Seymour Michael determined to withhold the news for his own reasons. Dora was to be kept in the dark because she was a woman, and therefore unsafe.

This was the plan in its original shape with which Michael sought out Arthur Agar at his rooms in college at Cambridge. It was further assisted and elaborated by a circumstance which the originator could scarcely have been expected to foresee - the fact of Arthur Agar's love for Dora, which was at this time beginning to take to itself a definite existence. It began, as all love does, with a want more or less elevated according to the nature of the wanter. Arthur Agar required some one for whom to buy those small and feminine luxuries which he could not for manly shame purchase to himself. He delighted in spending money in those establishments tersely called *magasins de luxe* in the country from whence their contents do emanate. He therefore got into the habit of "picking up little things" for Dora, with the result that she in her turn picked up that very small object, his heart.

Michael had seen enough of Arthur Agar during this short interview to endow him with the same need of contempt which he had entertained towards Anna Agar, the mother. The strong personal resemblance, the obvious weakness of the boy's face, and, above all, that sense of having the upper hand, which makes brave men out of cowards, gave him confidence. It seemed that he had only to play the cards thrust into his hand.

"I knew," he pursued, "Jem Agar very well. He was a peculiar man: very quiet, very reserved, and just the man to make a difficult position rather more difficult."

Arthur's intelligence was not keen enough to follow the drift of this remark.

"Yes," he said gently.

"He hinted to me once or twice," went on Seymour Michael, "that things were not very harmonious at home."

"I was not aware of it," answered Arthur, whose innate gentlemanliness told him that this should be held sacred ground.

The General shifted his position.

"He was a first-rate soldier," he said warmly.

It was obvious to both that they were not getting on. Something seemed to hold them both back, paralysing the *savoir-faire* which both had acquired in their intercourse with the world. Seymour Michael was puzzled. He was not afraid of this boy. He knew himself to be stronger - capable of over-mastering him entirely. But for the first time in his life he felt awkward and ill at ease.

Arthur Agar only wanted this man to go. He felt that he could forego the news which he must undoubtedly be in a position to give if only he could be rid of this hated presence. At moments the loathing came to him again, like a cold hand laid upon his heart.

"Were you with him," inquired the undergraduate, "at the time of his - death?"

"No. I was at head-quarters, forty miles to the rear."

There was a little pause, then suddenly Seymour Michael leant forward with his two hands on the table that stood between them.

"Mr. Agar," he said, "are you able to keep a secret?"

"I suppose so," answered Agar apprehensively.

"Then I am going to tell you something which you must swear by all that you hold most sacred to keep a strict secret until such time as I give you leave to reveal it."

Arthur looked at him with a vague fear in his face. It seemed suddenly as if this man had always been in his life - as if he would never go out of it again.

"I am not sure that I care to hear it," he wavered.

"You must hear it. Almost the last words that Jem Agar spoke to me were requesting me to tell you this."

"You promise that that is true?"

Arthur was surprised at his own suspicions. It was so

unlike him, whose nature, too weak to compass vice, had never allowed the suspicion of vice or deceit in others to trouble him.

"I promise," replied Seymour Michael.

Arthur gathered himself together for an effort. His distrust of this man was almost a panic.

"Then tell me," he said.

Michael leant back in his chair, fixing his pleasant eyes on Arthur's pale face.

"The estate is not yours," he said. "Your step-brother, Jem Agar, is not dead."

"Not dead!" repeated Arthur, without any joy in his voice. "Not dead! Then who are you? Tell me who you are!"

"Ah! That I cannot tell you."

And Seymour Michael sat smiling quietly on Anna Agar's son.

CHAPTER XVI

THE SPIDER AND THE FLY

How oft the sight of means to do ill deeds
Makes ill deeds done!

He is a wise liar who makes use of the truth at times.
Seymour Michael was clever enough to stay his
fantastic tongue in his further explanation to Arthur
Agar.

"It is a long story," he said, "and in order to fully state
the case to you I must go into some matters of which
perhaps you have heard little. Do you happen to be
anything of a politician? Are you, I mean, interested in
foreign affairs?"

Arthur confessed that he knew nothing of foreign
affairs, a fact of which Michael had become fully
aware on entering the narrow-minded, characteristic
room.

"You perhaps know," Seymour Michael went on, in a
tone of which the sarcasm was lost upon its victim,
"that Russia is living in hopes of some day possessing
India?"

"Oh - ah - yes!"

Arthur Agar was obviously not at all interested. There were so many things of a similar nature to be remembered - things which did not really interest him - and those nearer home had precedence in his mind. He knew, for instance, that Trinity Hall lived in hopes of heading the river that year, and that the Narcissus Club were going to give a narcissus-coloured dance in May week, at which entertainment even the jellies were to be yellow.

The General now launched into an explanation, couched carefully in language suitable to his hearer's limited knowledge of the facts.

"Russia," he said, "is now so large that, unless they make it larger still and get tropical resources to draw upon, it will fall to pieces. They want India. Some day there will be a fight, a very large fight. But not yet. In the meantime it is a question of learning every inch of that country where the battle-fields will be, and every thought in the minds of those men who will look on at the fight. I -"

He paused, recollecting that the fame of his own name might have penetrated even to this out-of-the-way spot. "Some of us have been at this all our lives. Over there, on the Frontier, there are certain numbers of us, on both sides, playing a very deep game. Your brother is one of the players, a prominent man on the field; a half-back, one might call him."

There was a strong temptation to continue the allegory - to say that he himself was goal-keeper; but Seymour Michael was one of the few men who can in need make even their own vanity subservient to convenience.

Henry Seton Merriman

"We watch each other," he went on, "like cats. We always know where the others are, and what they are doing. Your brother was one of the most closely watched by the other side. For some time we have been aware of an influence at work with a tribe of Hillmen who have hitherto been friendly to us, and we have not been able to find what this influence is, or how it is brought to bear upon them. We were so closely watched that we could not penetrate to the affected country. But at last the chance came. Your brother was gazetted as killed. We allowed the report to remain uncontradicted. We let the other side think that Jem Agar was dead, and therefore incapable of doing any more harm, and now he has gone up into that country to find out what they are after."

Arthur nodded.

"I see," he said. He was rather vague about it all, and had not quite realised yet that this was all true, that this man whom he still hated and distrusted without any apparent reason was real and living, speaking to him in real waking life and not in a dream. Moreover, he had not nearly realised that Jem was alive. The evidence of his own black clothes, of the sombre-edged stationery, of his mourning habit of life this term, was too strong upon a mind like his to be suddenly thrown aside. Perhaps he had discovered that the consolation of inheritance was greater than was at first apparent. In six weeks he had slipped very comfortably into Jem's shoes, and it seemed only right and proper that his life should have a background of the noble proportions of Stagholme. Also, now Stagholme meant Dora; for he was worldly-wise enough to know that his own personal value in the world's estimation had undergone a great change in six short weeks. He knew that the man with the money usually wins.

It would almost seem that Seymour Michael divined his thoughts, at least in part.

"There are two reasons," he went on to say, "why absolute secrecy is necessary; first, for Agar's own sake. He is, of course, in disguise. No one suspects that he is there, and that is his only safeguard in the country where he is. Secondly - but I want your whole attention, please."

"Yes, I am listening."

Seymour Michael leant forward and emphasised his remark by tapping on the table with his gloved finger.

"The mission is so extremely dangerous that it comes almost to the same thing."

"What do you mean?" inquired Arthur Agar, whose gentle intellect only compassed subtleties of the drawing-room type.

"I mean that Jem Agar is almost as good as a dead man, although he was not killed at Pregalla."

The man who had wept in this same room six weeks before looked up with a gleam of something very like hope in his troubled eyes. Such is the power of love. For Arthur Agar had not been ignorant of the probability that in his step-brother, once dead but now living, he had had a rival. Sister Cecilia had seen to that.

"But when shall we know? When will he come back?"

inquired he. And Seymour Michael, the subtle, began to see his way more clearly.

"Certainly not for six months, probably not for nine."

One may take it that no man is sent into the world a ready-made scoundrel. It all depends upon the circumstances of life. No one is safe right up to the end, and events may combine to make the very best of us into that thing which the world calls a villain.

Arthur Agar, all inexperienced, weak, hereditarily handicapped, suddenly found himself on the balance. And the scales were held, not by the hand of Justice, blind and clement, but by Seymour Michael, very open-eyed, with a keen watchfulness for his own purpose; biassed; unscrupulous. It must be admitted that circumstances were against Arthur Agar.

"There is nothing to be done," added Seymour Michael, with a smile which his companion could not be expected to fathom, "but to keep very quiet, and to make the best of your opportunities while you occupy the position of heir."

Arthur smiled in a sickly way. He felt suddenly as if this man could see right through him, and all the while he hated him. Seymour Michael meant "debts" - it was only natural that one of his race should think of money before all things - Arthur's thoughts were fixed on Dora. And guiltily he imagined himself to be detected.

"You will be doing no harm to Jem," said the tempter, with his pleasant laugh. "You are called upon to act the part well for his sake."

"Ye-es, I suppose I am," answered Arthur. "And I must tell no one?"

"Absolutely no one."

Despite his credulous nature, Arthur Agar was singularly suspicious on this occasion.

"Are these Jem's own instructions?" he asked.

"His own instructions," replied Seymour Michael callously.

Arthur paused in deep reflection. It was evident, he argued to himself, that Jem could not have cared for Dora, or he would never have left her in ignorance of the truth. If, therefore, during Jem's absence, he could win Dora for himself, he could not in any way be accused of wronging his step-brother. And we all know that a conscience which argues with itself is lost.

"To make things easier for us both," pursued Seymour Michael, "I propose that this interview remain a strict secret between ourselves, and for that purpose I have suppressed my own name. It is a fairly well-known name. I may mention that in guarantee of good faith. As, however, you do not know me, it will be easier for you to suppress the fact that we have ever met."

Arthur almost laughed at these last words. It seemed as if he had known this man all his life - as if his whole existence had merely been a period of waiting until he should come.

"And my mother must not know?" he said. He kept harking back to this question with a singular persistence. There are a few men and many women for whom a secret is a responsibility to be transferred to the first-comer without hesitation. One half of the world takes pleasure in divulging a secret - for the other half it is positive pain to keep one.

Seymour Michael never dreamt that the secret might be in unsafe hands. To a secretive man like himself the incapacity to keep a counsel never suggested itself. There is no doubt that where we all err is in persistently judging others by ourselves. Arthur Agar was keenly aware of his own incompetence in many things - he was one of those promising undergraduates who hire a man to water six small plants in a window-box. Incompetence was by him reduced to a science. There were so many things which he could not do, that he was forced to find occupations for a very extensive leisure, and these were usually of the petty accomplishment order, which are graceful in young girls and very disgraceful in young men.

Now the doctrine of incompetence is a very dangerous one. Already in the criminal courts we are beginning to hear of men and women who do not feel competent to keep the law. There were many laws of social procedure and a few of schoolboy honour which Arthur Agar felt to be beyond him, and he considered that in making confession he was acquiring a right to absolution.

He did not tell General Michael that he was not good at keeping secrets, chiefly because that gentleman was not of the trivial confession type; but he made a mental reservation.

Seymour Michael had risen and was walking

backwards and forwards slowly between the window and the door. He seemed quite at home in the small room, and his manner of taking three strides and then wheeling round suggested the habit of living in tents.

"What you must say is that you have received your brother's effects," he said. "If they ask from whence - from the War Office. I am the War Office to all intents and purposes. The affair is almost forgotten. All the details have been published - the usual newspaper details, with Fleet Street local colouring. You should have no difficulty."

"No," answered Arthur meekly, but with another mental reservation.

"There are, of course, certain legal formalities in progress," went on the General, "relative to the estate. Those must be allowed to go on. We may trust the lawyers to go slowly. And afterwards they can amuse themselves by undoing what they have done. That is their trade. Half of them make a living by undoing what the others have done. You are ..."

Seymour Michael so far forgot himself as to pause and make a mental calculation. Arthur saw him do it and never thought of being surprised. It seemed quite natural that this man should possess data upon which to base mental calculations.

"... not twenty-one yet?" Michael finished the sentence.

"No."

"So that, you see, they cannot make over the estate to

you before the time your brother comes or - should - come - back."

Arthur understood the emphasis perfectly this time. He was getting on.

"There are," continued Michael, who was eminently methodical, "a few military formalities, which have had my attention. In fact, I think that everything has been attended to. In case you should require any information, or perhaps advice, write to C 74, Smith's Library, Vigo Street. That is the address on that envelope."

Arthur rose too. The thought that his visitor might be about to depart thrilled through him with the warmth of relieved suspense.

"For your own information," said Michael, looking straight into the wavering, colourless eyes, "I may tell you that in my opinion - the opinion of an expert - this expedition is exceedingly hazardous. We - we must be prepared for the worst."

Arthur Agar turned away. He had felt the deep eyes probing his very soul - looking right through him. A sickening sense of weakness was at his heart. He felt that in the presence of this man he did not belong to himself.

"You mean," he muttered awkwardly, "that Jem will never come back?"

"I think it most probable. And then - when we have to abandon all hope, I mean - we shall be glad that we kept this thing to ourselves."

Seymour Michael held out his hand, and pressed the boy's weak fingers in a careless grip. Then he turned, and with a short "Good-bye" left him.

Arthur stood looking at the closed door with the frightened eyes of a woman. He looked round at the familiar objects of his room - the futile little gimcracks with which he had surrounded an existence worthy of such environments - the invitation cards on the draped mantelpiece, the little glass vases of fantastic shape with a single bloom of stephanotis, the hundred and one fantasies of a finicking generation wherein Art sappeth Manhood. And his eyes were suddenly opened to a new world of things which he could not do. He gazed - not without a vague shame - into a perspective of incompetencies.

In the *laissez-aller* of the unreflective he had assumed that life would be a continuance of small pleasures and refined enjoyments, little dinners and pleasant converse, Dora and a comfortable home, mutual mild delight in flowers and table decoration. Into this assumption Seymour Michael had suddenly stepped - strong, restless, and mysterious - and Arthur became uneasily conscious of possibilities. There might be something in his own life, there might even be something within himself, over which he could have no control. There was something within himself - something connected with the man who had gone, leaving unrest behind him, as he left it wherever he passed. What was this? Whither would it lead?

Arthur Agar rang the bell, and kept the "gyp" in the room on some trivial pretext. He was afraid of solitude.

CHAPTER XVII

TWO MOTIVES

Making vain pretence
Of gladness, with an awful sense
Of one mute shadow watching all.

"Pooh! the girl is happy enough!"

Mr. Glynde jerked his newspaper up and read an advertisement of steamships about to depart to the West Coast of Africa. His wife - engaged in cutting out a scarlet flannel garment of diminutive proportions (an operation which she made a point of performing on the study table) - gave two gentle snips and ceased her occupation.

She looked at the back of her husband's head, where the hair was getting a little thin, and said nothing. No one argued with the Reverend Thomas Glynde.

"The girl is happy enough," he repeated, seeking contradiction. There are times when an autocrat would very much like to be argued with.

"She is always lively and gay," he continued defiantly.

"Too gay," Mrs. Glynde whispered to the scissors, with

a flash of the only wisdom which Heaven gives away, and it is not given to all mothers.

The winter had closed over Stagholme, the isolating, distance-making winter of English country life, wherein each house is thrown upon its own resource, and the peaceful are at rest because their neighbours cannot get at them.

Dora was out. She was out a good deal now; exceedingly busy in good works of a different type from those affected by Sister Cecilia. The winter air seemed to invigorate her, and she tramped miles with a can of soup or an infant's flannel wrapper. And always when she came in she was gay, as her father described it. She gave amusing descriptions of her visits among the cottagers, retailed little quaint conceits such as drop from rustic lips declared unto them by their fathers from the old time before them, and in it all she displayed a keen insight into human nature. At times she was brilliant; which her father noticed with grave approval, ignorant or heedless of the fact that brilliancy means friction. Happy people are not brilliant.

She suddenly developed a taste for politics, and read the newspaper with a keen interest. Several half-forgotten duties were revived, and their performance became a matter of principle.

Mr. Glynde did not notice these subtle changes. Old men are generally selfish, more so, if possible, than young ones, and Mr. Glynde was eminently so. He only saw other people in relationship to himself. He looked at them through himself.

Mrs. Glynde had taken the opportunity of a "cutting

out" to mention that she thought a change would do Dora good. During the three months that had elapsed since the announcement of Jem's death, Stagholme had necessarily been a somewhat dull abode. The winter had not come on well, but in fits and starts, with trying winds and much rain. She said these things while she cut into her roll of red flannel - the scissors seemed to give her courage.

The Rector of Stagholme had awful visions of a furnished house at Brighton or a crammed hotel on the Riviera.

"Where do you want to go to?" he inquired, with a gruffness which meant less than it conveyed.

"To town, dear."

Now Mr. Glynde loved London.

In the meantime Dora was standing at the gate of the gamekeeper's little cottage-garden which adjoined the orchard at Stagholme. There were certain women with whom Sister Cecilia did not "get on," and these were by tacit understanding relegated to Dora. This same inability to "get on" was one of the crosses which Sister Cecilia carried in a magnified condition through life. The gamekeeper's wife was one of the failures - a hardy mother of several hardy little embryo game-keepers, who held that she knew her own business of motherhood best, and intimated as much to Sister Cecilia.

Dora went there very frequently, and the pathos of her way with little children is one of the things which cannot be touched upon here. It is possible that she went there because the cottage was near the Holme, and the way took her past the great house. She had never laid aside her old girlish habit of passing through the rooms, unannounced, to exchange a few words with Mrs. Agar. It was not that she held that lady in great veneration or respect; but in the country people learn to take their neighbours as they are, remembering that they are neighbours.

She went through the orchard and in at the side-door, which stood always open to the turn of the handle. She had fallen into a singular habit of always using this entrance, and of glancing as she passed at the stick-rack, where a rough mountain-ash was wont to stand - a stick which Jem had cut, while she stood by, years before. There was, perhaps, something characteristically suggestive of Jem in this stick - something strong and simple. She was not the person to indulge in sentimental thoughts; she could not afford to do that, Indeed, she often looked into the stick-rack without thinking, but she never passed it without looking.

In the library she found Mrs. Agar, talking to her maid, who withdrew with a pinched salutation. Mrs. Agar was one of those unfortunate women who level all ranks in their sore need of a listener. The expression of her face was decidedly lachrymose.

"Poor Arthur!" she exclaimed. "Dora, dear, something so dreadful has happened!"

"Yes," returned Dora, with the indifference of one who has tasted of the worst.

"Poor Arthur has received Jem's papers and diaries and things, and I can see from his letter that it has quite

Henry Seton Merriman

upset him. He is so sympathetic, you know."

Dora had turned quite away. She usually carried a stick in her country rambles, and it seemed suddenly to have suggested itself to her to lay this on a table near the door. The stick fell off again, and some moments elapsed while she picked it up from the floor. When she turned, her veil had slipped from the brim of her hat down over her face.

"But it could not have been a surprise to him," she said quietly. "He must have known that there would probably be something of the sort sent home."

"Yes, yes. But you know, dear, how keenly he feels everything. These highly-strung, artistic temperaments - but I need not tell you; you know Arthur almost as well as I do."

Dora answered nothing. It was not the first time that Mrs. Agar had charged some remark with that weight of significance which, in her vulgar-minded subtlety, she considered delicate and exceptionally clever. And each time that Dora heard it she was conscious of a vague discomfort, as at the approach of some danger, of some interference in her life which would be too strong for her to resist. It was one of those mean feminine thrusts to parry which is to acknowledge, to ignore is to admit fear.

"Has he sent them on to you?" she asked after a little pause, resisting only by a great effort the temptation to look towards the writing-table.

"Yes," was the reply. "It appears that they have been in his possession for some time. He kept them back for some reason - I cannot think why."

Providence is sometimes unexpectedly kind. Had Mrs. Agar been a different woman, had she, perhaps, been a better woman, less aggravating, more discreet, more honourable, she would not have done at this moment precisely that which Dora was silently praying that she would do.

"Here," continued the mistress of Stagholme, going to the writing-table, "is his diary; perhaps you would care to look through it? Poor Jem! I am afraid it will not be very interesting."

Dora took the little dark-coloured book almost indifferently.

"Thanks," she said. "It was always an effort to him to write the very shortest letter, was it not? Papa would like to see it, I know, if I may show it to him."

Being rather taller than Mrs. Agar, she could see over that lady's shoulder as she stood turning over with some curiosity a score or so of bundles evidently containing letters.

"These," said Mrs. Agar, "seem to be letters; probably our letters to him. Shall we burn them?"

Dora reflected for a moment. She knew that many of the bundles must contain letters from herself to Jem - letters which could have been read from the housetops without conveying anything to the populace. But some of them - almost between the lines - had been intended to convey, and had conveyed, something to Jem. She reflected - without anger, as women do on such matters - that if curiosity moved her, Mrs. Agar would not scruple to open all these letters and read them. The packets had evidently not been opened, and a momentary feeling of grateful recognition of Arthur's gentlemanly honour passed through her mind. There was about the faded papers that dim, mysterious odour which ever clings to packages that have been packed in India.

"Yes," she said, "let us burn them."

Mrs. Agar seemed to hesitate for a moment, but it was only for effect. She dreaded the packages, for one of them might contain the will which haunted her.

And so these two women, so very different, from such very different motives, carried the letters to the fire, and there they burnt them. In the curling flames Dora saw her own handwriting. She could not understand the suppressed excitement of Mrs. Agar's manner; she only knew that the mistress of Stagholme seemed to be afraid of looking at the burning papers.

When all was consumed both women heaved a sigh of relief.

"There," said Mrs. Agar, "I am glad we have been able to save poor Arthur that. These things are so very painful."

Dora looked rather as if she could not understand why the painful things of life should be harder for Arthur to bear than for other people. But she said nothing.

"He will be glad," continued Mrs. Agar, "to hear that it was you who helped me. I know he would rather that it had been you than any one."

All this with the horrid meaning, the sly significance, of her kind; for there are women for whom there is absolutely nothing sacred in the whole gamut of human feelings. There are women who will talk of things upon which the lips of even the most depraved men are silent.

And with it there was nothing that Dora could take exception to - nothing that she could answer without running the risk of bringing upon herself questions to which she had no reply.

"Well," she said cheerfully, "it is done now, so we can dismiss it from our minds. Of course you know that mother is getting out of hand altogether. I cannot hold her in. Her plans are simply kittenish. She wants to take a flat in town for two months, to take Boulton and one maid, to hire a cook, and to go generally to the bad."

Mrs. Agar's eyes glistened. She liked to hear of other people seeking excitement because she felt more justified in doing so herself.

"Well, I think she is very sensible. I am sure you all want a change. I feel I do. It is so depressing here all alone with one's thoughts. Sister Cecilia was just saying the other day that I ought to go away to Brighton or somewhere - that I owed it to Arthur."

"I don't see why you should not pay it to yourself, whoever you owe it to," said Dora. "This is an age of going away for changes. Life is like old Martin's trousers - so patched up with changes that the original pattern has disappeared."

"Yes, dear," replied Mrs. Agar, with a vague laugh. In conversation with Dora she invariably felt clumsy and unable to protect herself, like a stout fencer conscious of many vulnerable outlying points. She did not understand this girl, and never knew which was carte and which tierce. "So you are going away?"

"I expect so. Mother usually carries through her little schemes, and in his inward soul papa is rather a fast old gentleman. He loves the pavement, and - I don't object to the shops myself."

"Then you will like it?"

"Oh yes!" replied Dora, rising to go. "Like Mr. Martin, I am not sure that the old pattern is worth preserving."

"I wish I could go with you," said Mrs. Agar, holding up her cheek in an absent way for the farewell kiss; "I have not been to town for ages."

"Last week," amended Dora mentally.

"Why not come too?" she said aloud, gathering together stick, basket, and gloves.

"There is Arthur," replied the lady. "I am afraid he will not care to leave home just now, after so great a blow."

"All the more reason why he should go to town for a little and forget - himself."

Mrs. Agar smiled sadly and waited for further persuasion. She had fully made up her mind to go to

Brighton, but was anxious first that the whole parish should press her to do so against her will.

"It will be very nice," continued Dora, "to have you to help me to keep my flighty progenitors in order. Now I *must* go."

With a nod and a light laugh she closed the library door behind her, having apparently forgotten the sadder events of the visit. But in her basket she had the diary.

CHAPTER XVIII

LIKE SHIPS UPON THE SEA

Be as one that knoweth, and yet holdeth his tongue.

"And, of course, you know every one in the room?" Dora was saying to her cousin as the orchestra struck suddenly into "God bless the Prince of Wales."

"Good gracious, no!" Miss Mazerod replied; and both young ladies stood up to curtsey to the Royal party.

It was the great artistic *soirée* of the year, and crowds of nobodies jostled each other in their mad desire to deceive whosoever might be credulous into the belief that they were somebodies.

"Of course," said Dora, when they were seated again, and the strains of the Welsh air had been suppressed "by desire," "they may be very great swells; I have no doubt they are in their particular way; but they do not look it."

Miss Mazerod looked round critically.

"Some of them," she said, "are frame-makers, a good many of them, with big bills in high places. Others are actresses - very great actresses off the stage. Do you see that tall girl there, with a supercilious expression which she does not know is apt to remind one of a housemaid scorning a milkman's love on the area steps? She is a great actress, who will not take small engagements, and is not offered large ones. She is an actress 'pour se faire photographier.'"

"And this is the cream of London society?" said Dora, looking round her with considerable amusement.

"Society," returned her cousin, "is not allowed to stand for cream now. It is stirred up with a spoon, silver-gilt, and the skim milk gets hopelessly mixed up with the cream. That young man who is now talking to the actress person is not what he looks. He is, as a matter of fact, the scion of a noble house, who models in clay atrociously."

"And the gorgeous person he is turning his back upon?"

"One of his models."

"Of clay?"

"Essentially so."

And Miss Mazerod broke off into a happy laugh. Hers was not the bitterness of plainness or insignificance, but something infinitely more suggestive. It was, indeed, not bitterness at all, but light-hearted contempt, which is, perhaps, the deepest contempt there is.

"Who is the wretched woman with no backbone draped in rusty black?" asked Dora.

"My dear! That is one of the great lady artists of the age. She lectures to factory girls or something, and she paints limp females snuffling over tiger-lilies. Her ideal woman has that sort of droop of the throat - I imagine she-tries to teach it to the factory. She objects to backbone."

Miss Mazerod, who possessed a very firm little specimen of the adjunct mentioned, drew herself up and smiled commiseratingly.

"Then," said Dora, "I feel quite consoled about my sketches."

For the first time Miss Mazerod looked serious.

"Dora," she said, "I often wonder whether it would be profane to mention in one's prayers a little gratitude for not having an artistic soul. There are lots of women like that in the world, especially in London. They pretend that they think themselves superior to men, but they know in their hearts that they are inferior to women. For they have not something that women ought to have - No, Dolly, no brown studies here; you must not dream here!"

Dora, with a light laugh, came back from her mental wanderings to find herself looking at a face which caught her attention at once. It was the face of a man - brown, self-contained, with unhappy eyes and a long drooping nose.

"Who is *that* man?" she inquired at once. "Now, he is quite different from the rest. He is about the only person who is not furtively finding out how much attention he has succeeded in attracting."

"Yes, that is a man with a purpose."

"What purpose?" inquired Dora.

"I don't know; I shouldn't think any one knows."

"*He* knows," suggested Dora.

"Yes, *he* knows."

Miss Mazerod was looking at the mechanism of her fan with a demure expression on lips shaped for happiness. A dark young man was elbowing his way through the mixed crowd towards them.

"What is his name?" asked Dora, who was still looking at the man with a purpose.

"General Seymour Michael."

"The Indian man?"

"Yes."

There was a little pause, during which Miss Mazerod glanced in the direction of the younger man, who had been detained by a stout lady with a purple dress and a depressed daughter.

"I should like to know him," said Dora.

"Nothing easier," replied her cousin, still absorbed in the fan. "I know him quite well."

"He is looking at you now."

Miss Mazerod looked up and bowed with a little jerk, as if she felt too young to be stately; one of those bows that say "Come here."

At this moment the younger man came up and shook hands effusively with Dora, slowly with Miss Mazerod.

"Jack," said that young lady, "I have just beamed on General Michael, who is behind you. I want to introduce him to Dora."

Jack seemed to think this an excellent idea, and stepped aside with alacrity.

Seymour Michael came forward with his pleasant smile. He certainly was one of the most distinguished-looking men in the room, with a brilliant ribbon across his breast, and that smart, well-brushed general effect which stamps the successful soldier.

"When did you come back to England?" inquired Edith Mazerod, whose father had worked with this man in India.

"I - oh! I have been home six months," he replied, shaking hands with a subtle *empressemant* which was more effective than words.

"On leave?"

"No. Laid on the shelf."

He stood upright, drawing himself up with ironical emphasis, as if to show as plainly as possible that there were many years of life and work in him yet.

Edith Mazerod laughed, the careless passing laugh of inattention.

"Dora," she said, "may I introduce General Michael? My cousin."

She rose, and Seymour Michael prepared to take the vacant seat. The youth called Jack was making signs with his eyebrows, and in attempting to decipher his meaning she forgot to mention Dora's name.

"You will be sorry for this," said Seymour Michael, sitting down. "You will not thank your cousin."

"Why?" inquired Dora, prepared to like him, possibly because he had a brown face and wore his hair cut short.

"Because," he replied, "I am hopelessly new to this work."

"So am I," replied Dora; "I don't even know what pictures to look at and what to ignore. So I dare not look at the walls at all."

"That is precisely my position, only I am worse. You know how to behave in polite circles; I don't. You have a slightly tired look, as if this sort of thing wearied you by reason of its monotony."

"Have I? I am sorry for that."

"No, there is no reason to be sorry. They all have it."

"But," protested Dora, "I am not one of them. I am only aping the Romans."

"You do it well; I shall study your method. You do it better than Edith Mazerod."

"Edith is young - hopelessly, enviably young. Do you know them well?"

"Yes, I knew them in India."

"Of course; I forgot."

He turned and looked at her sharply. Sometimes his own reputation, far from being a happiness, gave him cause for misgiving. A man with an unclean record cannot well be sure that all the details he would wish suppressed have been suppressed. There was a little pause, during which they both watched the self-satisfied throng moving in and out, here and there, full of a restless desire to be observed.

It was Seymour Michael who spoke first. True to his mixed blood, he sought to make himself safe.

"Excuse me," he said, "but Edith Mazerod did not mention your name; may I ask it?"

"Dora Glynde!"

She saw him start. She saw a sudden wavering gleam in his eyes which in another man she would have set down to fear.

"Miss Dora Glynde," he repeated; and the expression of his face was so serene again that the look which had passed away from it began already to present itself to her memory as a conception of her own brain.

"When I was younger and shyer," he said, with a singular haste, "I was afraid to ask a lady her name when I did not catch it, and - and I frequently regretted not having had the courage to do so."

She recollected it all afterwards - every word, every pause. But then, as so frequently happens, knowledge aided her memory, and added significance to every detail.

"Are you staying with the Mazerods?" he asked.

"Yes, I am being shown life. I am doing a season. To-night is part of my education. To-morrow, I believe, we go to Hurlingham; the next day to a charity bazaar, and so on. I believe I am getting on very well. Aunt Mary is pleased with me. But I still stare about me, and show visible disappointment when I am presented to a literary celebrity or some other person of newspaper renown."

"Celebrities in the flesh *are* disappointing."

"Not only that, but I find that many of them are just a little common. Not quite what we in the country call gentlemen."

"Ah! Miss Glynde, you forget that Art rises superior to class distinctions."

"Yes, but artists don't; and artists' wives don't rise at all. I think you are to be congratulated. In your profession there are fewer persons 'superior to class distinction.'"

This was a subject which Seymour Michael dreaded.

He was ignorant of how much Dora might know. He had suspected from the first that Jem Agar's desire that she should know the truth had been a mere matter of sentiment; but the fact of meeting her at this public festivity, gay and in colours, shook this theory from its foundation. He disliked Edith Mazerod, because he suspected that his own early career had probably been discussed in her hearing, and her easy lightness of heart was to him as incomprehensible as it was suspicious. Dora he rather feared without knowing why.

"I suppose you know India well?" she said, looking straight in front of her.

"Too well," was the reply, with a sharp sidelong glance.

He was right. At that moment Dora might have been one of these *habituées* of rout and ballroom. She was very pale and looked tired out.

"I went out there thirty years ago," he continued, "into the Mutiny. From that time to this India has been killing my friends."

There was a little pause. She knew that in the natural course of events it was almost certain that this man knew Jem personally. It would have been easy to mention his name; but the wound was too fresh, her heart was too sore to bear the sting of hearing him discussed.

For a second Seymour Michael hovered on the brink. His lips almost framed the name. Good almost triumphed over evil.

And the girl sitting there - broken-hearted, quiet and strong, as only women can be - never knew how near she was. Sometimes it seems as if the cruelty of fate were unnecessary, as if the word too little or the word too much, which has the power to alter a whole life, were withheld or spoken merely to further a Providential experiment.

"Yes," said Michael, "I hate India."

And the spell was broken, the moment lost for ever. Seymour Michael had kept silence, and elsewhere, perhaps, at that very moment his doom was spoken. Who can tell? We are offered chances - we are, if you will, the puppets of an experiment - and surely there must be a moment which decides.

Dora was conscious of having miscalculated her own strength. She had led him on to the dangerous ground, but it was with relief that she saw him step back. She did not dare to lead him to it again.

It was not long before he left her, on the timely arrival of another friend.

The introduction brought about by Miss Mazerod did not seem to have been an entire success, for they parted gravely and without a word expressing the hope of meeting again. And yet Dora liked him, for he was strong and purposeful, such as she would have had all men. She wanted to know more of him. She wanted to be admitted further into the knowledge which she knew to be his.

Seymour Michael was conscious of a feeling of discomfort, no less disquieting by reason of its vagueness. He had a nervous sensation of being surrounded by something - something in the nature of a chain, piecing itself together, link by link - something that was slowly closing in upon him.

CHAPTER XIX

AT HURLINGHGAM

I must be cruel only to be kind.

It is not your deep person who succeeds in carrying out a set purpose, but one who is just profound enough to be fathomed of the multitude. For, after all, the multitude is ready enough to help, in a casual, parenthetic way, in the furtherance of a design; and a little depth, serving to flatter that vanity which taketh delight in a sense of superior perspicacity, only adds to the zest. There are plenty of people ready to pull on a rope or shove at a wheel, but there are more eager to do so if they are offered the direction of affairs.

Mrs. Glynde was one of those easily-fathomed persons who often succeed in their designs by the very transparency of their method. She had come to London with the purpose of leaving Dora there under the care of her sister Lady Mazerod, and before she had talked to that amiable widow for half an hour the design was as apparent as if it had been spoken.

In due course Dora and Miss Mazerod renewed a childish love, and at the end of April Mr. And Mrs. Glynde went back to Stagholme alone. It is probable that neither Mrs. Glynde nor Providence could have chosen a better companion for Dora at this time than Edith Mazerod. There was a breezy simplicity about this young lady's view of life which seemed to have the power of simplifying life itself. There are some people like this to whom is vouchsafed a limited comprehension of evil and an unlimited belief in good. A very shrewd author, who is, perhaps, not so much read to-day as he ought to be, said that "to the pure all things are pure." He often said less than he meant. For he knew as well as we do that the pure-minded are just so many moral filters who clear the atmosphere and take no harm themselves.

Dora Glynde required some one like this; for she had, as the French say, "found herself." The little world of Stagholme - the world of this Record - was intensely human. There was nobody very good in it and nobody very bad. Jem, with that quicker perception of evil which is wisely included in the mental outfit of men, had warned her against Sister Cecilia. And she had begun to understand his meaning now. Mrs. Agar she had found out for herself. Her father she respected and loved, but she had reached that age wherein we discover that father and mother are but as other men and women. Her mother she loved with that half-patronising affection which is found where a daughter is mentally superior.

The only person whom she had ever really respected and looked up to without reserve was Jem.

Altogether life was too complicated, subtle, difficult, hopeless, when Edith Mazerod came into it, and by her presence seemed to clear the atmosphere of daily existence.

At first the constant round of visiting and gaiety was a supreme effort; then came tolerance, and finally that business-like acceptance which is mistaken by many for enjoyment. The human machine is not constructed to go always at high pressure, either in happiness or in misery. We cannot exist all day and all night with a living care on our shoulders - the greatest misery slips off-sometimes. With men it can be lubricated by hard work, and likewise by alcohol, but the latter method is not always to be advised. With women there is much consolation to be extracted from a new dress or several new dresses and a hat. Even a new pair of gloves may help a breaking heart, and a glass of bitter beer taken at the right moment (with or without faith) has power to change a man's view of life.

So Dora, who had at no time been tragic, began to find that Academy *soirées* and similar entertainments assisted her in preserving towards the world that attitude which she had elected to assume. And if there be any who blame her, they are at liberty to do so. It is not worth while to pause for the purpose of writing - on the ground or elsewhere - for their edification.

Only one such alleviation did she repent of in after life. The day after the Academy *soirée* the Mazerods took her to Hurlingham. And Hurlingham became one of the pages of her life which she would have wished to tear completely out.

When they drove in through the simple gateway and round by the winding drive, it was evident that a great afternoon was to be expected. The blue-and-white club flag fluttered over a pavilion crammed from roof to terrace. The teams were already out in their bright colours, curveting about, each with a practice ball, on their stiff little ponies, moving with that singular cramped action only seen on the polo ground.

It was one of those brilliant days in early May when only gardeners, grumbling, talk or think of rain. A few fleecy white clouds seemed painted. So motionless were they, on the sky, reproducing the Hurlingham colours far above the ground. A gentle breeze coming up from the river brought with it the odour of lilac and budding things.

The chairs were crowded with a well-dressed throng, the larger majority of which seemed to be unaware that polo was the object of the afternoon.

The Mazerods and Dora had scarcely taken chairs when Arthur Agar presented himself. His tailor had apparently told him that after a lapse of six months it was permissible to assume habiliments of a slightly resigned tenour. His grey suit was one of the most elegant on the ground, his Suède gloves fitted perfectly, his tie was unique. And Arthur Agar was as happy as the best-dressed girl there.

The reception accorded him was not exactly enthusiastic. Having in view the fact that the young man called Jack was entirely satisfactory, Lady Mazerod treated all other young men with indifference. Edith despised Arthur Agar because Jack was athletic in his tendencies; and Dora was sorry to see him, because she had not answered his three last letters. There were also numerous small but expensive presents for which she had failed to tender thanks.

Unfortunately the young man called Jack turned up at tea-time, carrying one of the heavy chairs, which never fail to spoil the gloves of some of us, with unconscious ease. Owing to the activity and enterprise of this young gentleman, tea was soon procured, and consequently despatched before the interval was over and before the band had wet its whistle with something of a different nature from that in vogue on the lawn. A stroll through the gardens was proposed, and Lady Mazerod sent the young people off alone. There was no choice; but Dora had probably no thought of making a choice, had such been offered to her. She, like many another young lady, erred in placing too great a confidence in her own powers of staving things off.

There was no doubt whatever about Edith and the energetic John. They led the way round by the river path and the tennis-courts with a sublime disregard for the eye of the multitude, leaving Dora and Arthur to follow at such speed as their discretion might dictate.

Before they had left the tennis-lawn Arthur plunged. It may have been the desperation of diffidence, or perhaps that the new grey suit and the unique tie lent him confidence. One sees a young lady completely carried off her mental status by the success of a dress or the absence of a dreaded competitor, and Arthur Agar had enough of the woman in him to give way to this dangerous vertigo.

"Dora," he said, "you have not answered my last three letters."

"No," she replied, "because they struck me as a little ridiculous."

"Ridiculous!" he repeated, with such sincere dismay that she was moved to compassion. " Ridiculous ,

Dora, why?"

His horror-struck, almost tearful voice gave her a pang
of self-reproach, as if she had struck some defenceless
dumb animal.

"Well, there were things in them that I did not
understand."

"But I could make you understand them," he said, with
a sudden self-assertion which startled her. The weakest
man is, after all, a man - so far as women are
concerned.

"I think you had better not," she said, hurrying her
steps.

But he refused to alter his pace, and he disregarded her
warning.

"They meant," he said, "that I wanted you to know that
I love you."

There was a little pause. Dora was struck dumb by a
chill sense of foreboding. It was like a momentary
glance into a future full of trouble.

"I am sorry," she said, "for that. I hope - that you may
find that it is a mistake."

"But it is not a mistake. I don't see why it should
be one."

Dora paused. She was afraid to strike. She did not
know yet that it is less cruel to be cruel at once.

"It is best to look at these things practically," she said. "And if we look at it practically we shall find that you and I are not at all likely to be happy together."

"However I look at it, I only see that I should never be happy without you."

"Then, Arthur, you are not looking at it practically."

"No, and I don't want to," he replied doggedly.

"That is a mistake. A little bit of life may not be practical, but all the rest of it is; and for the gratification of that little bit, there is all the rest to be lived through."

Arthur looked puzzled. He rearranged the orchid in his coat before replying. He had found time to think of the orchid.

"I don't understand all that," he said. "I only know that I love you, and that I should be miserable without you. Besides, if that little bit is love - I suppose you admit there is such a thing as love?"

Dora winced. She was looking through the trees across the peaceful evening river.

"Yes," she answered gently. "I suppose so."

Arthur Agar had been brought up in an atmosphere of futile discussion, but he had never wanted anything in vain. There are women - fools - who dare to bring up children thus in a world where wanting in vain is the chief characteristic of daily life. Arthur was ready enough to go on discussing his future thus, but never doubted that it would all come to his desire in the end. He was like a woman in so much as he failed to understand an argument which he could not meet.

They walked on amidst the flowering shrubs, and Dora was filled with a disquieting sense of having failed to convince him.

"I do not want to hurry you," said Arthur presently, with a maddening equanimity. "You can give me your answer some other time."

"But I have given it now."

Arthur was engaged in taking off his hat to a passing lady, and made no acknowledgment of this.

"Everybody at home would be pleased," he observed, after a pause occupied by the adjustment of his hat. "They all want it."

It was not that he refused to take No when it was given to him, but rather that he did not recognise it, never having encountered it before.

They were now coming round by the pigeon-shooting enclosure, and the strains of the band announced that the interval for tea had elapsed.

In the distance Lady Mazerod and Edith, attended by the indefatigable Jack, were keeping a chair for Dora. She slackened her pace. To her the knowledge had come that the difficulties of life have usually to be met single-handed. She was not afraid of Arthur, but this was a distinct difficulty because of the influence he had at his back.

"Arthur," she said, "I think we had better understand each other *now*. It may save us both something in the future. I cannot help feeling rather sorry that I must say No. Every girl must feel that. I do not know from whence the feeling comes. It is a sort of regret, as if something good and valuable were being wasted. But, Arthur, it *is* No, and it must always be No. I am not the sort of person to change."

"I suppose," he replied, *en vrai fils de sa mère*, "that there is some one else?"

He turned as he spoke, but Dora's parasol was too quick for him.

"Please do not let us be like people in books," she said. "There is no necessity to go into side issues at all. You have asked me to marry you. I can never marry you. There is the whole question and the whole answer. I say nothing to you about finding somebody worthier, or any nonsense of that sort. Please spare me the usual - impertinences - about there being somebody else."

The word found its mark. Arthur Agar caught his breath, but made no answer.

They were among the well-dressed throng now crowding back to the chairs.

When Arthur had handed Dora over to the care of Lady Mazerod he lifted his hat and took his departure with that perfect *savoir faire* which was his *forte*.

CHAPTER XX

IN A SIDE PATH

"To sum up all, he has the worst fault-a husband can have, he's not my choice."

There is something doubtful in a love-making that is in more than two pairs of hands. This is a day of syndicates. The strength that lies in union is cultivated nowadays with much assiduity. But in matters of love the case is not yet altered, and never will be. It is a matter for two people to decide between themselves, and all interference is mistaken and deplorable. It is usually, one notices, those persons who are incapable of the feeling themselves who seek to interfere in the affairs of others.

That one of the principals should seek aid in such interference proves without appeal that he does not know his business. Such aid as this Arthur Agar had sought. He had, as Dora suspected, written to his mother, with full particulars of the conversation beneath the Hurlingham trees. He had laid before her many arguments, which, by reason of their effeminacy, appealed to her illogical mind, proving that Dora could not do better than marry him. The arrangement, he argued, was satisfactory from whatever point of view it might be taken; and, finally, he begged his mother to try and succeed where he had failed. He did not propose that Mrs. Agar should appeal to Dora; not because such a course was repellent, but merely because he knew a better. He suggested that Mrs. Agar should sound Mr. Glynde upon the matter.

This suggestion was in itself a stroke of diplomacy. The astute have no doubt found out by this time that the Reverend Thomas Glynde loved money; and a man who loves money has not the makings of a good father within him, whatever else he may have. Whether Arthur was aware of this it would be hard to say. Whether he had the penetration to know that, in the nature of things, Mr. Glynde would urge Dora to marry Arthur Agar and Stagholme, without due regard to her own feelings in the matter, is a question upon which no man can give a reliable opinion. Certain it is that such a course was precisely what the Reverend Thomas had marked out for himself.

He had an exaggerated respect for money and position - a title was a thing to be revered. Clergymen, like artists, are dependent on patronage, and must swallow their pride. It is therefore, perhaps, only natural that Mr. Glynde should be quite prepared to make some sacrifice of feeling or sentiment (especially the feeling and sentiment of another) in order to secure a position.

Arthur Agar simply followed the spirit of the age. He could not succeed alone, and therefore he proceeded to form a syndicate to compel Dora to love him, or in the meantime to marry him.

"Of course," said Sister Cecilia to Mrs. Agar, when the matter was first under discussion, " she would soon learn to care for him. Women *always* do."

Which shows how much Sister Cecilia knew about it.

"And besides, I believe she cares for him already," added Mrs. Agar, who never did things by halves.

Sister Cecilia dropped her head on one side and looked convinced - to order.

"Of course," pursued Mrs. Agar vaguely, "I am very fond of Dora; no one could be more so. But I must confess that I do not always understand her."

Even to Sister Cecilia it would not do to confess that she was afraid of her.

The interview was easily brought about. Mrs. Agar wrote a note to the Rector and asked him to luncheon. The Rector, who had not had many legal affairs to settle during his uneventful life, was always pleased to be consulted upon a subject of which he knew absolutely nothing. Besides, they gave one a good luncheon at Stagholme in those days.

"I have had a letter from dear Arthur," said Mrs. Agar, at a moment which she deemed propitious, namely, after a third glass of the Stagholme brown sherry.

"Ah! I hope he is well. The boy is not strong."

"Yes, he is quite well, thank you. But of course he has had a great shock, and one cannot expect him to get over it all at once."

The Rector did not hold much by sentiment, so he

contented himself with a grave sip of sherry.

"And now I am afraid there is fresh trouble," added Mrs. Agar.

"Been running into debt?" suggested Mr. Glynde.

"No, it is not that. No, it is Dora."

"Dora! What has Dora been doing?"

Mrs. Agar was polishing the rim of a silver salt-cellar with her forefinger.

"Of course," she said, "I have seen it going on for a long time. My poor boy has always - well, he has always admired Dora."'

"Oh!"

"Yes, and of course I should like nothing better. I am sure they would be most happy."

The Rector looked doubtful.

"We must not forget," he said, "that Arthur is constitutionally delicate. That extreme repugnance to active exercise, the love of ease and - er - indoor pursuits, show a tendency to enfeeble the organisation which might - I don't say it will, but it might - turn to decline."

"But the doctors say that he is quite strong. Everybody cannot be robust and - and massive."

She was thinking of Jem, against whom she had

always borne a grudge, because his inoffensive presence alone had the power of making Arthur look puny.

"No; and of course with care one may hope that Arthur will live to a ripe old age," said the Rector, who was only coquetting with the question.

Mrs. Agar played with a biscuit. She had a rooted aversion to the query direct.

"I should have thought," she said, "that you or her mother would have seen that such an attachment was likely to form itself."

The truth was that the Reverend Thomas did not devote very much thought to any subject which did not directly influence his own well-being. He had at one time thought that an attachment between Jem and Dora might conveniently result from a childhood's friendship, but Arthur had not entered into his prognostications at all. He rather despised the youth, as much on his own account as that he was Anna Agar's son.

"Can't say," he replied, "that the thing ever entered my head. Of course, if the young people have settled it all between themselves, I suppose we must give them our blessing, and be thankful that we have been saved further trouble."

He thought it rather strange that Dora should have fixed her affections on such an unlikely object as Arthur Agar; but it was part of his earthly creed that the feelings of women are as incomprehensible as they are unimportant. Which, by the way, serves to show how very little the Rector of Stagholme knew of the world.

"But," protested Mrs. Agar, "they have *not* settled it between themselves. That is just it."

"Just what?"

"Just the difficulty."

Immediately Mr. Glynde's face fell to its usual degree of set depression.

"What do they want me to do?" he inquired, with that air of resignation which is in reality no resignation at all.

"Well," said Mrs. Agar volubly, "it appears that Arthur spoke to Dora at Hurlingham, and for some reason she said No. I can't understand it at all. I am sure she has always appeared to like him very much. It may have been some passing fancy or something, you know. When she is told that it would please us all, perhaps she will change her mind. Poor Arthur is terribly cut up about it. Of course a man in his position does not quite expect to be treated cavalierly like that."

Mr. Glynde smiled. Behind the parson there was somewhat even better; there was a just and honest English gentleman, which, in the way of human species, is very hard to beat.

"I am afraid Arthur will have to manage such affairs for himself. When a girl is settling a question involving her whole life she does not usually pause to consider the position of the man who asks her to be his wife. He would have no business to ask her had he no position, and the rest is merely a matter of degrees."

"Then you don't care about the match?" said Mrs. Agar, to whose mind the earliest rudiments of logic were incomprehensible.

"I do not say that," replied the Rector, with the patience of a man who has had dealings with women all his life; "but I should like it to be understood that Dora is quite free to choose for herself. I am willing to tell her that the match would be satisfactory to me. Arthur is a gentleman, which is saying a good deal in these days. He is affectionate, and, so far as I know, a dutiful son. I have little doubt he would make a good husband."

Mrs. Agar wiped away an obvious tear, which ran off Mr. Glynde's mental epidermis like water off the back of the proverbial fowl. This also he had learnt in the course of his dealings with the world.

"He has been a good son to me," sniffed the fond and foolish mother.

Neither of these persons was capable of understanding that "goodness" is not all we want in husband or wife. These good husbands - heaven help their wives! - break as many hearts as those who are labelled by the world with the black ticket.

"Then I may tell Arthur that you will help him?" said Mrs. Agar, with a sudden access of practical energy.

"You may tell him that he has my good wishes, and that I will point out to Dora the advantages of - acceding to his desire. There are, of course, advantages on both sides, we know that."

As usual, Mrs. Agar overdid things. The airiness of her indifference might have deceived a child of eight, provided that its intellect was not *de première force.*

"Ye-es," she murmured, "I suppose Dora would bring her little - eh - subscription towards the household expenses. Sister Cecilia gave me to understand that there was a little something coming to her under her mother's marriage settlement."

Mrs. Agar was not clever enough to see that she had made a mistake. The mention of Sister Cecilia's name acted on the Rector like a mental douche. He was just beginning to give way to expansiveness - probably under the suave influence of the brown sherry - and the name of Sister Cecilia pulled him together with a jerk. The jerk extended to his features; but Mrs. Agar was one of those cunning women whom no man need fear. She was so cunning that she deceived herself into seeing that which she wished to see, and nothing else.

"All that," said the Rector gravely, "can be discussed when Arthur has persuaded Dora to say Yes."

He was in the position of an unfortunate person who, having come into controversy with the police, is warned that every word he says may be used in evidence against him. He had been reminded that every detail of the present conversation would be repeated to Sister Cecilia, with embellishments or subtractions as might please the narrator's fancy or suit her purpose.

"A dangerous woman" he called Sister Cecilia in his most gloomy voice, and a parson must perforce fear dangerous women. That is one of the trials of the ministry.

Mrs. Agar laughed in a forced manner.

"Of course," she said - she had a habit of beginning her remarks with these two words - "of course, we need not think of such questions yet. I am sure all *I* want is the happiness of the dear children."

"Umph!" ejaculated Mr. Glynde, who was not always a model of politeness.

"That, I am sure," continued Mrs. Agar, with a dabbing pocket-handkerchief, "is the dearest wish of us all."

"When does the boy come home?" inquired the Rector.

"Oh, in a week. I am so longing for him to come. He has to go to town to get some clothes, which will delay his return by one night."

"Is he doing any good this term?"

Mrs. Agar looked slightly hurt.

"Well, he always works very hard, I am only afraid that he should overdo it. You know, I suppose, that he did not get through his examination this term. Of course it is no good *my* saying anything, but I am quite convinced that they are not dealing fairly by him. I have seen some of those examination papers, and some of the questions are simply spiteful. They do it on purpose, I know. And Sister Cecilia tells me that that *does* happen sometimes. For some reason or other - because they have been snubbed, or something like that - the masters, the examiners, or whatever they are called, make a dead set at some men, and simply keep them back. They don't give them the marks that they ought to have. Why should Arthur always fail? Of course the thing is unfair."

This theory was not quite new to the Rector. He had given up arguing about it, and usually took refuge in flight. He did so on this occasion. But as he walked home across the park, smoking a cigarette, he reflected that to the owner of Stagholme such a small matter as a college career was, after all, of no importance. These broad acres, the stately forests, the grand old house, raised Arthur Agar above such considerations, indeed above most considerations. And Mr. Glynde made up his mind to put it very strongly to Dora.

CHAPTER XXI

ALONE

The name of the slough was Despond.

When Dora returned to Stagholme a fortnight later she was relieved to find that Arthur had not yet come down from Cambridge.

It is a strange thing that in the spring-time those who are happy - *pro tempore*, of course, we know all that - are happier, while those who carry something with them find the burden heavier. Stagholme in the spring came as a sort of shock to Dora. There were certain adjuncts to the growth of things which gave her actual pain. After dinner, the first night, she walked across the garden to the beechwood, but before long she came back again. There is a scent in beech forests in the spring which is like no other scent on earth, and Dora found that she could not stand it.

Her father and mother were sitting in the drawing-room with open windows, for it was a warm May that year. She came in through the falling curtains, and something warned her to keep her face averted from the furtive glance of her mother's eyes. She had learnt something of the world during her brief season in town, and one of the lessons had been that the world sees more than is often credited to it.

"The worst," she said cheerfully, "of a season in town is that it makes one feel aged and experienced. Middle age came upon me suddenly, just now, in the garden."

Mr. Glynde was looking at her almost critically over his newspaper.

"How old are you?" he asked curtly.

"Twenty-five."

In some indefinite way the question jarred horribly. Dora was conscious of a faint doubt in the infallibility of her father's judgment. She knew that in a worldly sense he was more experienced, more thoughtful, cleverer than her mother, but in some ways she inclined towards the maternal opinion on questions connected with herself.

At this moment Mrs. Glynde was called from the room, and went reluctantly, feeling that the time was unpropitious.

Mr. Glynde's life had been eminently uneventful. Prosperous, happy in a half-hearted, almost negative, way, somewhat selfish, he had never known hardship, had never faced adversity. It is such men as this who love what they call a serious talk, summoning the subject thereof with exaggerated gravity to a study, making a point of the *mise en scène*, and finally saying nothing that could not have been spoken in course of ordinary conversation.

Dora detected the odour of a serious talk in the

Henry Seton Merriman

atmosphere, and she found that something had taken away the awe which such conversations had hitherto inspired. It may have been the season in town, but it was more probably that confidence which comes from the knowledge of the world. There were things in life of which she consciously knew more than her father, and one of these was sorrow. There is nothing that gives so much confidence as the knowledge that the worst possible has happened. It raises one above the petty worries of daily existence.

Dora knew that her acquaintance with sorrow was more intimate, more thorough, than that of her father, who sat looking as if the hangman were at the door. She awaited the serious talk with some apprehension, but none of that almost paralysing awe which she had known in childhood.

"I am getting an old man," he said, with supreme egotism, "and you cannot expect to have me with you much longer."

"But I do expect it," replied Dora cheerfully. "I am sorry to disappoint you, papa, but I do expect it most decidedly."

This rather spoilt the lugubrious gravity of the situation.

"Well, thank Heaven! I am a hearty man yet," admitted the Rector rather more hopefully; "but still you cannot expect to have your parents with you all your life, you know."

"I think it is wiser not to look too far into the future," replied Dora, warding off.

"I should look much more happily into the future," replied the Rector, with the deliberation of the domestic autocrat, "if I knew that you had a good husband to take care of you."

In a flash of thought Dora traced it all back to Arthur, through Mrs. Agar; and her would-be lover fell still further in her estimation. He seemed to be fated to show himself at every turn the very antitype to her ideal.

"Ah," she laughed, "but suppose I got a bad one? You are always saying that marriage is a lottery, and I don't believe the remark is original. Suppose I drew a blank; fancy being married to a blank! Or I might do worse. I might draw minus something - minus brains, for instance. They are in the lottery, for I have seen them, nicely done up in faultless linen - both blanks and worse."

She turned away towards the window, and the moment her face was averted it changed suddenly. The face that looked out towards the beech-wood, where the shadows were creeping from the darkening east, was piteous, terror-stricken, driven.

It is an ever-living question why people - honest, well-meaning parents and others - should be set to ride rough-shod over all that is best and purest in the human mind.

The Rector went on, in his calmly self-satisfied voice, with a fatuous ignorance of what he was doing which must have made the very angels wince.

"A great many girls," he said, "have thrown away a

chance of happiness merely to serve a passing fancy. Mind you don't do that."

She gave a little laugh, quite natural and easy, but her face was grave, and more.

"I do not think there is any fear of that," she replied lightly. "You must confess, papa, that I have always displayed a remarkable capacity for the management of my own affairs - with the assistance of Sister Cecilia, *bien entendu.*"

This was rather a forlorn hope, but Dora was driven into a corner. The Rector was in the habit of preaching a good methodical sermon, and usually finished up somewhere in the neighbourhood of the text from whence he started. He allowed himself to deviate, but he never turned his back upon his text and went for a vague ramble through scriptural meadows, as some have been heard to do. He deviated on this occasion for a moment, but never lost sight of the main question.

"Sister Cecilia," he said, "is a busybody, and, like all busybodies, a fool. It is always people who cannot manage their own affairs who are so anxious to help their neighbours. I have no doubt that you are as capable of looking after yourself as any girl; but, child, you must remember that experience goes a long way in the world, and in the nature of things I must know better than you."

"Of course you do, papa dear. I know that."

But she did not know it, and he knew that she did not. This knowledge is certain to come, sooner or later, to men and women who have lived for themselves and in themselves alone. They are mental hermits, whose opinion of things connected with the lives of others cannot well be of value because they have only studied their own existences.

The Rector of Stagholme suddenly became aware of this. He suddenly found that his advice was no longer law. There are plenty of us ready to confess that we cannot play billiards or whist or polo, but no man likes it to be known that he cannot play the game of life. Mr. Glynde did not like this subtle feeling of incompetency. He prided himself on being a man of the world, and frequently applied the vague term to himself. We are all men of a world, but it depends upon the size of that world as to what value our citizenship may be. Mr. Glynde's world had always been the Reverend Thomas Glynde. He knew nothing of Dora's world, and lost his way as soon as he set his foot therein. But rather than make inquiries he thought to support paternal dignity by going further.

"It is," he said, with inevitable egotism, "unnecessary for me to tell you that I have only your interests at heart."

"Quite, papa dear. But do not let us talk about these horrid things. I am quite happy at home, and I do not want to go away from it. There is nowhere in the world where I should sooner be than here, even taking into consideration the fact that you are sometimes the most dismal old gentleman on the face of the earth."

"Well," he answered, with a grim smile, "I am sure I have enough to make me dismal. I am thankful to say that there will be no difficulty about money. You will be well enough off to have all that you might desire.

But wealth is not all that a woman wants. She cannot turn it to the same account as a man. She wants position, a household, a husband. Otherwise the world only makes use of her; she is a prey to charity humbugs and bad people who do good works badly. I am not speaking as a parson, but as a man of the world."

"Then," she said, "as a parson, tell me if it would not be wrong to marry a man for whom one did not care, just for the sake of these things - a household and a husband."

"Of course it would," answered Mr. Glynde. "And that is a wrong which is usually punished in this life. But there are cases where it is difficult to say whether there be love or not. Unless you actually despise or hate a man, you may come to care for him."

"And in the meantime the position and the advantages mentioned are worth seizing?"

"So says the world," admitted Mr. Glynde.

"And what says the parson?"

She went to him and laid her two arms upon his broad chest, standing behind him as he sat in his arm-chair and looking down affectionately upon his averted face.

"And what says the parson?" she repeated, with a loving tap of her fingers on his breast.

"Nothing," was the reply. "A better parson than I says that what is natural is right."

"Yes, and that means follow the dictates of your own heart?"

"I suppose so," admitted the Hector, taking her two hands in his.

"And the dictates of my heart are all for staying at home and looking after my ancient parents and worrying them. Am I to be sent away? Not yet, old gentleman, not yet."

The Reverend Thomas Glynde laughed, somewhat as if a weight had been lifted from his heart. In his way he was a conscientious man. It was his honest conviction that Dora would do well to marry Arthur, who was a gentleman and essentially harmless. In persuading her to do so covertly, as he had thought well to do, he was honestly performing that which he thought to be his duty towards her. Presently Mrs. Glynde came back, and shortly afterwards Dora left the room. The Rector was not reading the book he held open on his knee, but gazed instead absently at the pattern of the hearthrug.

A change had come in this quiet household. Dora had gone away a child. She had come back a woman, with that consciousness of life which comes somewhere between twenty and thirty years of age - a consciousness which is partly made up of the knowledge that life is, after all, given to each one of us individually to make the best of as well as we may; and no one knows what that best is except ourselves. What is happiness for one is misery for another, and while human beings vary as the clouds of heaven, no life can be lived by set rule.

Over these things the Rector pondered. He felt the

difference in Dora. She was still his daughter, but no longer a child. Her existence was still his chief care, but he could only stand by and help a little here and there; for the dependency of childhood was left behind, and her evident intention was to work out her own life in her own way. So do those who are dependent by nature upon the advice and sympathy of others learn to lean only upon their own strength.

In the room overhead, standing by the window with weary eyes, Dora was murmuring: "I wonder - I wonder if I shall be able to hold out against them all."

CHAPTER XXII

ACROSS THE YEARS

Across the years you seem to come.

"That is just what I can't do. I cannot afford to wait."

Arthur Agar drew in his neatly-shod little feet, and leant back in the deep chair which was always set aside as his in the Stagholme drawing-room.

Mother and son were alone in the vast, somewhat gloomy apartment. Arthur had been home six hours, and the subject of their conversation was, of course, Dora.

Sister Cecilia was absent, only in obedience to a very unmistakable hint in one of Arthur's recent letters to his mother.

"Only a little while," pleaded Mrs. Agar. "Of course, dear, it will all come right. I feel convinced of that. Only you see, dear, girls do not like to be hurried in such an important step. I am quite sure she cares for you; only you *must* give her a little time."

"But I can't, I can't," he repeated anxiously. And his face wore that strangely accentuated look of trouble

Henry Seton Merriman

which almost amounted to dread - dread of something in life which had not come yet.

"Why not?" inquired Mrs. Agar. "You are both young enough, I am sure."

"Oh, yes, we are young enough."

He stirred his tea with an effeminate appreciation of fine Coalport and a dainty Norwegian spoon.

"Then why should you not wait?"

Arthur was silent; he looked very small and frail, almost childlike, in his silk-faced evening coat. Spoilt boy was writ large all over his person. "Arthur," said Mrs. Agar, "you are keeping something from me."

He shook his feeble head feebly.

"You are, I know you are. What is it?"

This was the only person in all the world who had stirred the heart of Anna Agar to something like a lasting affection. Once - years before - she had loved Seymour Michael with a sudden volcanic passion which had as suddenly turned to hatred. But under no circumstances could such a love have endured. Consistency, constancy, singleness of purpose were quite lacking in this woman's composition. It is rare, but when a woman does fail in this respect, her failure is more complete, more miserable than the failure of men, inconstant as they are.

Her affection for Arthur, coupled with that suspicion which always goes with a cheap cunning, had put her on the right scent.

"Tell me," she said, "I insist on knowing."

Still he held his peace, with the obstinate silence of the weak.

"Well, then," she cried, "don't ask me to help you to win Dora, that is all!"

There was a pause; in the silence of the great house the wind moaned softly. It always moaned in the drawing-room, whether in calm or storm, from some undiscovered draught in the high ventilated ceiling.

"I sometimes think," said Arthur at length, in an awestruck voice, "that Jem may not be dead."

"Not dead! Arthur, how can you be so stupid?"

She was not at all awestruck. Her denser, more sordid nature was proof against the silence or the humming wind. The greed of gain has power to kill superstition.

His face puzzled her. Suddenly he cast himself back and hid his face in his hands,

"Oh!" he muttered, "I can't do it, I can't do it!"

In an instant his mother was standing over him.

"Arthur," she hissed, "you *know* something?"

"Yes," he confessed in a whisper at length.

"Jem is not dead?" she hissed again. Her voice

was hoarse.

"He was not killed in the disaster," admitted Arthur. In his heart he was still clinging to the other hope subtly held out by Seymour Michael - the hope that in his simple intrepidity Jem had gone to his death.

"Then where is he - where is he, Arthur? Tell me quickly!"

Mrs. Agar was white and breathless. It was as if she had bartered her soul, and after payment, had been tricked out of her share of the bargain. She trembled with a fear which seemed to fill her world and extend to the other world to come.

"He escaped from that action," said Arthur, who, now that the truth was out, grew voluble like a child making a confession, "by being sent on in front with a few men. They escaped notice, while the larger body was attacked and massacred."

"Who told you this?"

"I do not know. I cannot tell you his name."

"Arthur!" exclaimed Mrs. Agar nervously, "are you going mad? Do you know what you are saying?"

In reply he gave a little laugh like a sob.

"Oh yes," he replied, "it is all right. I know what I am saying, though sometimes I scarcely believe it myself. If it was a hundred years ago one might believe it easily enough, but now it seems unreal."

"Then where is Jem? Was he taken prisoner? Those men are savages, aren't they? They kill - people when they take them prisoners."

"No, he was not taken prisoner," said Arthur. Sometimes he lost patience in a snappy, feminine way with his mother.

"Oh! tell me, tell me, Arthur dear! You are killing me!"

"I will, if you will let me. It appears that Jem had made himself a name out there for knowing the country and the people, which is useful to the Government, because Russia and England both want the country, or something like that; I don't quite understand it."

"Oh, never mind! Go on!" interrupted Mrs. Agar, with characteristic impatience.

"And at any rate the men on the other side - the Russians or some one, I don't know who - were in the habit of watching Jem so as to prevent his going up into this unexplored country. Well, when the report of his death was put in the newspapers it was left uncontradicted, so that these men should think he was dead, and not be on the look-out for him. Do you understand?"

Mrs. Agar had raised her head, with listening, attentive eyes. It seemed as if a voice had come to her across the years from the distant past. A voice telling an old story, which had never been forgotten, but merely laid aside in the memory among those things that never are forgotten.

Finding Arthur's troubled gaze upon her, she seemed to

Henry Seton Merriman

recollect herself with a little gesture of her hand to her breast as if breathing were difficult.

"That does not sound like a thing Jem would do," she said, with one of those flashes of shrewd observation which sometimes come to inconsequent people, and make it difficult for those around them to be sure how much they see and how much passes unobserved.

"It was not Jem, it was this other man."

"Which other man?" Mrs. Agar gave a little gasp, as if she had found something she feared to find.

"The man who told me - he was Jem's superior officer."

"When did he tell you - where?"

"He came to see me at Cambridge, and brought those things of Jem's," replied Arthur. So far from feeling guilty at thus revealing all that he had promised to keep secret, he was now beginning to experience some pangs of conscience at the recollection of a conceal-ment which, by a supreme effort, had been made to extend to four months.

There was a sly gleam in Mrs. Agar's eyes. A close observer knowing her well could have seen the cunning written on her face, for it was cheap and obvious.

"Oh!" she said indifferently, "and what sort of man was he?"

Arthur pondered with a deliberation that almost

maddened her.

"Oh!" he replied at length, "a small man, dark, with a sunburnt face; a Jew, I should think. He was rather well dressed - in the military style, of course."

"Yes," muttered Mrs. Agar. "Yes."

There was a long silence, during which Mrs. Agar reflected, as deeply, perhaps, as she had ever reflected in her life.

Then she discovered something for herself which had of necessity been pointed out to her son - a subtle divergence of character.

"But," she said, "of course Jem may never come back from this expedition. It *must* be very dangerous."

"It is very dangerous."

Mrs. Agar's sigh of relief was quite audible. It is thus that nature sometimes betrays human nature.

"Did *he* say that? Did *he* think that of it?"

Seymour Michael's opinion still had value in her eyes.

"Yes," the reply came slowly; "he said that we might almost look upon Jem as a dead man."

Mother and son looked at each other and said nothing. Heredity is a strange thing, and one alternately aggrandised and slighted. Blood is a very powerful force, but the little lessons taught in childhood's years bear a wondrous crop of good or evil fruit in later days.

Left alone, Arthur Agar's natural tendency was towards good. Probably because he was timid, and goodness seems the safer course. There are many who have not the courage to forsake goodness, even for a moment. But under the influence of a stronger will - that is to say, under the influence of four out of every five persons crossing his path - Arthur was liable to be led in any direction. He would rather have sinned in company than have cultivated virtue in the solitude usually accorded to that state.

Somehow, in his mother's presence it did not seem so very wrong to keep back the truth respecting Jem and to turn it to his own ends. It did not seem either mean or cowardly to take advantage of a rival's absence and gain his object, by deception. So, perhaps, it was in the beginning, when the world was young. In those days also a mother and son helped each other in deception, and so since then have many thousands of mothers (incompetent or vicious) led their children to ruin.

"Of course," said Mrs. Agar, "if Jem goes and does things of that description he must take the consequences."

Arthur said nothing in reply to this. The thought had been his for some months, but he had never put it into shape.

"We are perfectly justified," she went on, "in acting as if Jem were dead until he deigns to advise us to the contrary."

This also was putting a long-cherished thought into form.

Arthur knew that he ought to have told his mother then and there that Jem had taken every step in his power to advise him as soon as possible of the falseness of the news transmitted to the newspapers. But something held him silent, some taint of hereditary untruthfulness.

"I do not see," she said, "that this news can, therefore, make much difference. There is no reason to alter any of our plans. To begin with, I am certain that he is dead. We must have heard by this time if he had been living."

Arthur gave a little nod of acquiescence.

"And also," pursued Mrs. Agar, with characteristic inconsistency, "he evidently does not care about us or our feelings."

Arthur knew what she meant, and he descended as low in the moral scale as ever he went during his life.

"But," he said, "there is, all the same, no time to lose."

He passed his hand over his sleek, lifeless hair with a weary look.

"Well, dear," said his mother soothingly, "I will see Ellen Glynde to-morrow, and try to make her say something to Dora. A girl's mother has always more influence than her father."

This idiotic axiom seemed to satisfy Arthur, probably because he knew no better, and he rose to take his bedroom candlestick.

Mrs. Agar was a person utterly incapable of harbouring

two thoughts at the same moment. She never even got so far as to place two sides of a question upon an equal footing in her mind. All her questions had but one side. She was not thinking of Arthur when she went to her room. She was not thinking of him when she lay staring at the daylight, which had crept up into the sky before she closed her eyes.

She tossed and turned and moaned aloud with a childish impatience. Her mind could find no rest; it could not throw off the deadly knowledge that Seymour Michael had come back into her life. And somehow she was no longer Anna Agar, but Anna Hethbridge. She was no longer the fond mother whose whole world was filled by thoughts of her son - a miserable, thoughtless, haphazard world it was - but again she was the wronged woman, moved by the one great passion that had stirred her sordid soul, a fearsome hatred for Seymour Michael.

She was not an analytical woman; she had never thought about her own thoughts; she was as superficial as human nature can well be. That is to say, she was little more than an animal with the gift of speech, added to one or two small items of knowledge which divide men from beasts. But she *knew* that this was not the end. She never doubted for a moment that it was merely a beginning, that Seymour Michael was coming back into her life.

Like a child she tossed and tumbled in her bed, muttering half-consciously, "Oh, what shall I do? What shall I do?"

CHAPTER XXIII

AND THE TIME PASSES SOMEHOW

His hand will be against every man, and every man's hand against him.

For two days Mrs. Glynde had been going about the world with a bright red patch on either cheek; and it would seem that on the third day, namely, the Sunday, things came to a crisis in her disturbed mind. At morning service her fervour was something astonishing - the quaver in her voice was more noticeable in the hymns than ever, and the space devoted to silent prayer after the blessing was so abnormally long that Stark, the sexton, had to rattle the keys twice, with all due respect and for the sake of his Sunday dinner, before she rose from her knees; whereas once usually sufficed.

It was the devout practice that all the Rectory servants should go to evening service, while Mrs. Glynde, or Dora, or both, remained at home to take care of the house. On this particular evening Mrs. Glynde proposed that Dora should stay with her, and what her mother proposed Dora usually acceded to.

"Dear," said the elder lady, with a nervous little jerk of the head which was habitual or physical, "I have heard

Henry Seton Merriman

about Arthur."

They were sitting in the drawing-room, with windows open to the ground, and the fading light was insufficient to read by, although both had books.

"Yes, mother," answered the girl in rather a tired voice, quite forgetting to be cheerful. "I should like to know exactly what you heard."

"Well, Anna told me," and there was a whole world of distrust in the little phrase, "that Arthur had asked you to be his wife, and that you had refused without giving a reason."

"I gave him a reason," replied Dora; "the best one. I said that I did not love him."

There was a little pause. The two women looked out on to the quiet lawn. They seemed singularly anxious to avoid looking at each other.

"But that might come, dear; I think it would come."

"I know it would not," replied Dora quietly. There was a dreaminess in her voice, as if she were repeating something she had heard or said before.

Suddenly Mrs. Glynde rose from her chair, and going towards her daughter, she knelt on the soft carpet, still afraid to look at her face. There was something suggestive and strange in the attitude, for the elder woman was crouching at the feet of the younger.

"My darling," she whispered, "I know, I *know!* I have known all along. But mind, no one else knows, no one suspects! *It* can never come to you again in this life. Women are like that, it never comes to them twice. To some it never comes at all; think of that, dear, it never comes to them at all! Surely that is worse?"

Dora took the nervous, eager hands in her own quiet grasp and held them still. But she said nothing.

"I have prayed night and morning," the elder woman went on in the same pleading whisper, "that strength might be given you, and I think my prayers were heard. For you have been strong, and no one has known except me, and I do not matter. The strength must have come from somewhere. I like to think that I had something to do with it, however little."

Again there was a silence. Across the quiet garden, from the church that was hidden among the trees, the sound of the evening hymn came rising and falling, the harshness of the rustic voices toned down by the whispering of the leaves.

"I know," Mrs. Glynde went on, speaking perhaps out of her own experience, "that now it must seem that there is nothing left. I know that It can never come to you, but something else may - a sort of alleviation; something that is a little stronger than resignation, and many people think that it is love. It is not love; never believe that! But it is surely sent because so many women have - to go through life - without that - which makes life worth living."

"Hush, dear!" said Dora; and Mrs. Glynde paused as if to collect herself. Perhaps her daughter stopped her just in time.

"There is," she went on in a calmer voice, "a sort of satisfaction in the duties that come and have to be performed. The duties towards one's husband and the others - the others, darling - are the best. They are not the same, not the same as if - as they might have been, but sometimes it is a great alleviation. And the time passes somehow."

It is not the clever people who make all the epigrams; but sometimes those who merely live and feel, and are perhaps objects of ridicule. Mrs. Glynde was one of these. She had unwittingly made an epigram. She had summed up life in five words - the time passes somehow."

"And, dear," she went on, "it is not wise, perhaps it is not quite right, to turn one's back upon an alleviation which is offered. Arthur would be very kind to you. He is really fond of you, and perhaps the very fact of his not being clever or brilliant or anything like that might be a blessing in the future, for he would not expect so much."

"He would have to expect nothing," said Dora, speaking for the first time, "because I could give him nothing."

She spoke in rather an indifferent voice, and in the gloom her mother could not see her face. It was a singular thing that neither of them seemed to take Arthur Agar's feelings into account in the very smallest degree; and this must be accounted to them for wisdom.

Dora was, as her mother had said, very strong. She never gave way. Her delicate lips never quivered, but she took care to keep them close pressed. Only in her eyes was the pain to be seen, and perhaps that was why her mother did not dare to look.

"There is no hurry," she pleaded. "You need not decide now."

"But," answered Dora, "I have decided now, and he knows my decision."

"Perhaps after some time - some years?" suggested Mrs. Glynde.

"A great many years," put in Dora.

"If he asks you again - oh! I know it would be better, dear; better for you in every way. I do not say that you would be quite happy. But it would be a sort of happiness; there would be less unhappiness, because you would have less time to think. I do not say anything about the position and the wealth and such considerations, for they are not of much importance to a good woman."

"After a great many years," said Dora, in that calm and judicial voice which fell like ice on her mother's heart, "I will see - if he chooses to wait."

"Yes, but - " began Mrs. Glynde, but she did not go on. That which she was about to say would scarcely have been appropriate. But so far as the facts were concerned she might just as well have said it. For Dora knew as well as she did that Arthur Agar would not wait. Women are not blind to manifest facts. They know us, my brothers, better than we think. And they are not quite so romantic as we take them to be. Their love is a better thing than ours, because it is more practical and more defined. They do not seek an ideal of their own imagination; but when something approaching to it crosses their path in the flesh they know what they want, and they do not change.

Before the silence was again broken the murmur of voices told them that the church doors had been opened, and presently they discerned a female form crossing the lawn towards the open window. It was Sister Cecilia, walking with that mincing lightness of tread which seems to be the outward and visible sign of an inward and spiritual superiority over the remainder of womanhood. Good women - those mistaken females who move in an atmosphere of ostentatious good works - usually walk like this. Like this they enter the humble cot with a little soup and a lot of advice. Like this they smilingly step, where angels would fear to tread, upon feelings which they are incapable of understanding.

Mrs. Glynde got quietly up and left the room. As the door closed behind her Sister Cecilia's gently persuasive voice was heard.

"Dora! Dora dear!"

"Yes," replied the girl without any enthusiasm, rising and going to the window.

"Will you walk with me a little way across the fields? It is such a lovely evening."

"Yes, if you like."

And Dora passed out of the open window.

"I am sorry," said Sister Cecilia after a few paces, "that you were not in church. We had such a bright service."

Dora, like some more of us, wondered vaguely where the adjective applied, especially on a gloomy evening without candles, but she said nothing.

"I stayed at home with mother," she explained practically. "The servants were all out." Sister Cecilia was not listening. She was gazing up at the sky, where a few stars were beginning to show themselves.

"One feels," she murmured with a sigh, "on such an evening as this, that, after all, nothing matters much."

"About the servants do you mean? They are going on better now."

"No, dear, about life. I mean that at times one feels that this cannot be the end of it all."

"Well, we ought to feel that, I suppose, being Christians."

"And some day we shall see the meaning of all our troubles," pursued Sister Cecilia. "It is so hard for us older ones, who have passed through it, to stand by helpless, only guessing at the pain and anguish of it all, whereas, perhaps, we could help if we only knew. A little more candour, a little more confidence might so easily lead to mutual help and consolation."

"Possibly," admitted Dora, without any encouragement.

"I am so sorry for poor Arthur! " whispered Sister

Henry Seton Merriman

Cecilia, apparently to the evening shades.

Dora was silent. She knew how to treat Sister Cecilia. Jem had taught her that.

"It has been such a terrible blow. His letters to his mother are quite heartbroken."

Dora reserved her opinion of grown-up men who write heartbroken letters to their mothers.

"I know all about it," Sister Cecilia went on, quite regardless of the truth, as some good people are. "Dora, dear, I know all about it."

Silence, a silence which reminded Sister Cecilia of a sense of discomfiture which had more than once been hers in conversation with Jem.

"Have you nothing to tell me, dear?" she inquired. "Nothing to say to me?"

"Nothing," replied Dora pleasantly. "Especially as you know all about it."

"Will you never change your mind?" persuasively.

"No, I am not the sort of person to change my mind."

There was a little pause, and again Sister Cecilia whispered to the evening shades.

"I cannot help hoping that some day it may be different. It is not as if there were any one else -?"

Silence again.

"I dare say," added Sister Cecilia, after waiting in vain for an answer to her implied question, "that I am wrong, but I cannot help being in favour of a little more candour, a little mutual confidence."

"I cannot help feeling," replied Dora quietly, "that we are all best employed when we mind our own business."

"Yes, dear, I know. But it is very hard to stand idly by and see young people make mistakes which can only bring them sorrow. I want to tell you to think very deeply before you elect to lead the life of a single woman. It is a life full of temptation to idleness and self-indulgence. There are many single women who, I am really afraid, are quite useless in the world. They only gossip and pry into their neighbours' affairs and make mischief. It is because they have nothing to do. I have known several women like that, and I cannot help thinking that they would have been happier if they had married. Perhaps they did not have the chance. One does not understand these things."

Sister Cecilia cast her eyes upwards toward the tree-tops to see if perchance the explanation was written there.

"Of course," she went on complacently, drawing down her bonnet-strings, "there are many useful lives of single women. Lives which the world would sadly miss should it please God to take them. Women who live, not for themselves, but for others; who go about the world helping their neighbours with advice and the fruits of their own experience; ever the first to go to the afflicted and to those who are in trouble. They do not receive their reward here, they are not always thanked.

The ignorant are sometimes even rude. They have only the knowledge that they are doing good."

"That *must* be a satisfaction," murmured Dora fervently.

"It is, dear; it is. But - you will excuse me, Dora dear, if I say this? - I do not think you are that sort of woman."

"No," answered Dora, "I don't think I am."

"And that is why I have said this to you. Now, don't answer me, dear. Just think about it quietly. I think I have done my duty in telling you what, was on my mind. It is always best, although it is sometimes difficult, or even painful; but then, it is one's duty. Kiss me, dear! Good-night! - *good*-night!"

And so Sister Cecilia left Dora - mincing away into the gloom of the overhanging trees. And so she leaves these pages. Verily the good have their reward here below in a coat of self-complacency which is as impervious to the buffets of life as to the sarcasm of the worldly.

CHAPTER XXIV

A STAB IN THE DARK

Slander, meanest spawn of Hell;
And women's slander is the worst.

Mrs. Agar was a person incapable of awaiting that vague result called the development of things.

Arthur had never been forced to wait for anything in his life. No longer at least than tradespeople required, and in many cases not so long, for Mrs. Agar had an annoying way of refusing to listen to reason. She never allowed that laws applying to ordinary people, served more or less faithfully by tailor or dressmaker, applied to herself or to Arthur. And tradespeople, one finds are not always of the same mind as the Medes and Persians - they square matters quietly in the bill. They had to do it very quietly indeed with Mrs. Agar, who endeavoured strenuously to get the best value for her money all through life; a remnant of Jaggery House, Clapham Common, which the placid wealth of Stagholme never obliterated.

After the luncheon, specially prepared and laid before the Rector, this second Rebecca awaited the result impatiently. But nothing came of it. Although Mrs. Agar now looked upon Dora as the latest whim of the not-to-be-denied Arthur, she could hardly consider Mr. Glynde in the light of a tradesman retailing the said commodity, and, therefore, to be bullied and harassed into making haste. She reflected with misgiving that Mr. Glynde was an exponent of the tiresome art of talking over and thinking out matters which required neither words nor thought, and saw no prospect of an immediate furtherance of her design.

With a mistaken and much practised desire of striking when the iron was hot, Mrs. Agar, like many a wiser person, began, therefore, to bang about in all directions, hitting not only the iron but the anvil, her own knuckles and the susceptibilities of any one standing in the neighbourhood. She could not leave things to Mr. Glynde, but must needs see Dora herself. She had in her mind the nucleus of a simple if scurrilous scheme which will show itself hereafter. Her opportunity presented itself a few days later.

A neighbouring family counting itself county, presumably on the strength of never being able to absent themselves from the favoured neighbourhood on account of monetary incapacity, gave its annual garden-party at this time. To this entertainment the whole countryside was in the habit of repairing - not with an idea of enjoying itself, but because everybody did it. To be bidden to this garden-party was in itself a *cachet* of respectability. This indeed was the only satisfaction to be gathered from the festivity. If the honour was great, the hospitality was small. If the condescension was vast, the fare provided was verging on the stingy. Here were served by half-starved domestic servants, in the smallest of tumblers, "cups" wherein were mixed liquors, such as cider, usually consumed by self-respecting persons in the undiluted condition and in mugs. Upon cucumber-cup, taken in county society, as on a dinner of herbs, one hardly expects the guest to grow convivial. Therefore at this garden-party those bidden to the feast were in the habit of wandering sadly through the shrubbery seeking whom they might avoid, and in the course of such a perambulation, with a young man conversant of himself, Dora met Mrs. Agar. Even the mistress of Stagholme was preferable to the young man from London, and besides - there were associations. So Dora drew Mrs. Agar into her promenade, and presently the young man got his *congé*.

At first they talked of local topics, and Mrs. Agar, who had a fine sense of hospitality, said her say about the cider-cup. Then she gave an awkward little laugh, and with an assumption of lightness which did not succeed she said:

"I hope, dear, you do not intend to keep my poor boy in suspense much longer?"

"Do you mean Arthur?" asked Dora.

"Yes, dear. I really don't see why there should be this absurd reserve between us."

"I am quite willing," replied the girl, "to hear what you have to say about it."

"Yes, but not to talk of it."

"Well, I suppose Arthur has told you all there is to tell. If there is anything more that you want to know I shall be very glad to tell you."

"Well, of course, I don't understand it at all," burst out Mrs. Agar eagerly. This was quite true; neither she nor Arthur could understand how any one could refuse such a glorious offer as he had made.

"Perhaps I can explain. Arthur asked me to marry him. I quite appreciated the honour, but I declined it."

"Yes, but why? Surely you didn't mean it?"

"I did mean it."

"Well," explained Mrs. Agar, with a little toss of the head, "I am sure I cannot see what more you want. There are many girls who would be glad to be mistress of Stagholme."

And it must be remembered that she said this knowing quite well that Jem was probably alive. There are some crimes which women commit daily in the family circle which deserve a greater punishment than that meted out to a legal criminal.

"That is precisely what I ventured to point out to Arthur," said Dora, unconsciously borrowing her father's ironical neatness of enunciation.

"But why shouldn't you take the opportunity? There are not many estates like it in England. Your position would be as good as that of a titled lady, and I am sure you could not want a better husband."

"I like Arthur as a friend, but I could never marry him, so it is useless to discuss the question."

"But why?" persisted Mrs. Agar.

"Because I do not care for him in the right way."

"But that would come," said Mrs. Agar. It was only natural that she should use an argument which is accountable for more misery on earth than mothers dream of.

"No, it would never come."

Mrs. Agar gave a cunning little laugh, and paused so as to lend additional weight to her next remark.

"That is a dangerous thing for a girl to say."

"Is it?" inquired Dora indifferently.

"Yes, because they can never be sure, unless -"

"Unless what? I am quite sure."

"Unless there is some one else," said Mrs. Agar, with an exaggerated significance suggestive of the servants' hall.

Dora did not answer at once. They walked on for a few moments in silence, passing other guests walking in couples. Then Dora replied with a succinctness acquired from her father:

"Generalities about women," she said, "are always a mistake. Indeed, all generalities are dangerous. But if you and Arthur care to apply this to me, you are at liberty to do so. Whatever generalities you apply and whatever you say will make no difference to the main question. Moreover, you will, perhaps, be acting a kinder part if you give Arthur to understand once for all that my decision is final."

"As you like, dear, as you like," muttered Mrs. Agar, apparently abandoning the argument, whereas in reality she had not yet begun it.

"How do you do, dear Mrs. Martin?" she went on in the same breath, bowing and smiling to a lady who passed them at that moment.

"Of course," she said, returning in a final way to the question after a few moments' silence, "of course I do not believe all I hear; in fact, I contradict a good deal. But I have been told that gossips talked about you a good deal last year, at the time of Jem's death. I think it only fair that you should know."

"Thank you," said Dora curtly.

"Of course, dear, *I* didn't believe anything about it."

"Thank you," said Dora again.

"I should have been sorry to do so."

Then Dora turned upon her suddenly.

"What do you mean, Aunt Anna?" she asked with determination.

"Oh, nothing, dear, nothing. Don't get flurried about it."

"I am not at all flurried," replied Dora quietly. "You said that you would be sorry to have to believe what gossips said of me last year at the time of

Jem's death - "

"Dora," interrupted Mrs. Agar, "I never said anything against you in any way; how can you say such a thing?"

"And," continued Dora, with an unpleasant calmness of manner, "I must ask you to explain. What did the gossips say, and why should you be sorry to have to believe it?"

Mrs. Agar's reluctance was not quite genuine nor was it well enough simulated to deceive Dora.

"Well, dear," she said, "if you insist, they said that there had been something between you and Jem - long, long ago, of course, before he went out to India."

Dora shrugged her shoulders.

"They are welcome to say what they like."

Mrs. Agar was silent, awaiting a second question.

"And why should you be sorry to believe that?" inquired the girl.

"I - I hardly like to tell you," said Mrs. Agar, in a low voice.

Dora waited in silence, without appearing to heed Mrs. Agar's reluctance.

"I am afraid, dear," went on the elder lady, when she saw that there was no chance of assistance, "that we have been all sadly mistaken in Jem. He was not - all that we thought him."

"In what way?" asked Dora. She had turned quite white, and her lips were suddenly dry and parched. She held her parasol a little lower, so that Mrs. Agar could not see her face. She was sure enough of her voice. She had had practice in that.

"In what way was Jem not all that we thought him?" she repeated evenly, like a lesson learnt by heart.

Mrs. Agar stammered. She tried to blush, but she could not manage that.

"I cannot very well give you details. Perhaps, when you are older. You know, dear, in India people are not very particular. They have peculiar ideas, I mean, of morals - different from ours. And perhaps he saw no harm in it."

"In what?" inquired Dora gravely.

"Well, in the life they lead out there. It appears that there was some unfortunate attachment. I think she was married or something like that."

"Who told you this?" asked Dora, in a voice like a threat.

"A man told Arthur at Cambridge - one of poor Jem's fellow-officers. The man who brought home the diary and things."

Having once begun Mrs. Agar found herself obliged to go on. She had not time to pause and reflect that she was now staking everything upon the possibility of

Jem's death subsequent to the disaster in which he was supposed to have perished.

Dora did not believe one word of this story, although she was quite without proof to the contrary. Jem's letters had not been frequent, nor had they been remarkable for minuteness of detail respecting his own life. Mrs. Agar had done her best to put a stop to this correspondence altogether, and had succeeded in bringing about a subtle reserve on both sides. She had persistently told Jem that Dora was evidently attached to Arthur, and that their marriage was only the question of a few years. Of this Jem had never found any confirmatory hint in Dora's letters, and from some mistaken sense of chivalry refrained from writing to ask her point-blank if it were true.

"And why," said Dora, "do you tell me this? In case what the gossips said might be true?"

"Ye-es, dear, perhaps it was that."

"So as to save me from cherishing any mistaken memory?"

"Yes, it may have been that."

And Mrs. Agar was surprised to see Dora turn her back upon her as if she had been something loathsome to look upon, and walk away.

CHAPTER XXV

FROM THE JAWS OF DEATH

When the heart speaks, Glory itself is an illusion.

The *Mahanaddy* had just turned her blunt prow out westward from the harbour of Port Said, sniffing her native north wind, with a gentle rising movement to that old Mediterranean eastward-tending swell. The lights of the most iniquitous town on earth were fading away in the mist of the desert on the left hand, and on the right the gloom of the sea merged into a grey sky.

The dinner-hour had passed, and the passengers were lolling about on the long quarter-deck, talking lazily after the manner of men and women who have little to say and much time wherein to say it.

It was quite easy to perceive that they had left a voyage of many days behind them, for the funny man had exhausted himself and the politicians were asleep. The lifeless, homeward-bound flirtations had waned long ago, and no one looked twice at any one else. They all knew each other's dresses and vices and little aggravating habits, and only three or four of them were aware that human nature runs deeper than such superficial details.

Away forward, behind the sheep-pens, an Italian gentleman in the ice industry was scraping on a yellow fiddle which looked sticky. But like many things of plain exterior this unprepossessing instrument had something in it, something that the Italian gentleman knew how to extract, and all the ship was hushed into listening. Such as had conversation left spoke in low tones, and even the stewards in the pantry ceased for a time to test the strength of the dinner-plates.

On a small clear space of deck between the door of the doctor's cabin and the saloon gangway two men were walking slowly backwards and forwards. They were both tall men, both large, and consequently both inclined to taciturnity. They had said, perhaps, as little as any two persons on board, which may have accounted for the fact that they were talking now, and still seemed to have plenty to say.

One was dark and clean-shaven, with something of the sea in his mien and gait. His nose and chin were singularly clean cut, and suggestive of an ancestral type. This was the ship's doctor, a man who probed men's hearts as well as their bodies, and wrote of what he found there. His companion was an antitype - a representative of the fair race found in England by the ancestors of the other when they came and conquered. He wore a beard, and his face was burnt to the colour of mahogany, which had a strange effect in contrast to the bluest of Saxon eyes.

The Doctor was talking.

"Then," he was saying, "who the devil are you?"

The other smiled, a gentle, triumphant smile. The smile

of a man who, humbly recognising himself at a just estimation, is conscious of having outwitted another, cleverer than himself.

"You finish your pipe," he said, and he walked away with long firm strides towards the saloon stairs. The Doctor went to the rail, where, resting his arms on the solid teak, he leant, gazing thoughtfully out over the sea, which was part of his life. For he knew the great waters, and loved them with all the quiet strength of a slow-tongued man.

Before very long some one came behind and touched him on the shoulder. He turned, and in the fading light looked into the smiling face of his late companion - the same and yet quite different, for the beard was gone, and there only remained the long fair moustache.

"Yes," said Dr. Mark Ruthine, "Jem Agar. I was a fool not to know you at first."

A sort of shyness flickered for a moment in the blue eyes.

"I have been practising so hard during the last ten months to look like some one else that I hardly feel like myself," he said.

"Um-m! There was something uncanny about you when you first came on board. I used to watch you at meals, and wonder what it was. By God, Agar, I *am* glad!"

"Thanks," replied Jem Agar. He was looking round him rather nervously. "You don't think there is anybody on board who will know me, do you?"

"No one, barring the Captain."

"Oh," said Agar calmly, "he is all right. He can keep his mouth shut."

"There is no doubt about that," replied the Doctor.

A little pause followed, during which they both listened involuntarily to the ice-cream merchant's musical voice, which was now floating over the silent decks, raised in song.

"I should like to hear all about it some day," said the ship's surgeon at last. He knew his man, and no detail of the strange lives that passed the horizon of his daily existence was ever forgotten. Only he usually found that those who had the most to tell required a little assistance in their narration.

"It is rather a rum business," answered Jem Agar, not displeased.

At this moment the ship's bell rang four clear notes into the night.

"Ten o'clock," said the Doctor. "Come into my cabin and have a smoke; the Captain will be in soon. He would like to hear the story too."

So they passed into the cabin, and before they had been there many minutes the Captain joined them. For a moment he stood in the doorway, then he came forward with outstretched hand.

"Well," he said, "all that I can say is that you ought to be dead. But it's not my business."

He had seen too many freaks of fortune to be surprised at this.

"I thought," he continued, "that there was something familiar about the back of your head. Back of a man's head never changes. It's a funny thing."

He sat down in his usual chair, and looked with a cheery smile upon him who had risen from the death column of the *Times*. Then he turned to his pipe.

"You know, Agar," he said, "I was beastly sorry about that - death of yours. Cut me up wonderfully for a few minutes. That is saying a lot in these days."

Agar laughed.

"It is very kind of you to say so," he said rather awkwardly.

"And I," added Dr. Ruthine from behind the whisky and soda tray, in the deliberate voice of a man who is saying something with an effort, "felt that it was a pity. That is how it struck me - a pity."

Then, very disjointedly, and in a manner which could scarcely be set down here, Major James Agar told his singular story. There are - thank heaven! - many such stories still untold; there are, one would be inclined to hope, many such still uncommenced. As a nation we may be on the decline, but there is something to go on with in us yet.

Once when the narrator paused, Dr. Ruthine went to the side table and opened some bottles.

"Whisky?" he inquired, with curt hospitality, "or anything else your fancy may paint, down to tea."

Agar rose to pour out his own allowance, and for a moment the two men stood together. With the critical eye of a soldier, which seems to weigh flesh and blood, he looked his host for the time being up and down.

"They don't make men like you and me on tea," he said, reaching out his hand towards a tumbler.

Then the story went on. At first the ship's doctor listened to it with interest but without absorption, then suddenly something seemed to catch his attention and hold it riveted. When a pause came he leant forward, pointing an emphasising finger.

"When you spoke just now of the chief," he said, "did you mean Michael?"

"Yes."

"What! Seymour Michael?"

"Yes."

The Captain tapped his pipe against his boot and leant back with the shrug of the shoulders awaiting further developments.

"And you mean to tell me that you put yourself entirely in the hands of Seymour Michael?" pursued the Doctor.

"Yes, why not?"

Mark Ruthine shook his head with a little laugh. "I always thought, Agar, that you were a bit of a fool!"

"I have sometimes suspected it myself," admitted the soldier meekly.

"Why, man," said Ruthine, "Seymour Michael is one of the biggest rascals on God's earth. I would not trust him with fourpence round the corner."

"Nor would I," put in the Captain, "and the sum is not excessive."

Jem Agar was sipping his whisky and soda with the placidity of a giant who fears no open fight and never thinks of foul play.

"I don't see," he muttered, "what harm he can do me."

"No more do I, at the moment," replied the Doctor; "but the man is a liar and an unscrupulous cad. I have kept an eye on him for years because he interests me. He has never run a straight course since he came into the field; he has consistently sacrificed truth, honour, and his best friend to his own ambition ever since the beginning."

Jem Agar smiled at the Doctor's vehemence, although he was aware that such a display was far from being characteristic of the man.

"Of course," he admitted, "in the matter of honour and glory I expect to be swindled. But I don't care. I know the chap's reputation, and all that, but he can hardly get rid of the fact that I have done the thing and he has not."

"I was not thinking so much of that," replied the other. "Men sell their souls for honour and glory and never get paid."

He paused; then with the sure touch of one who has dabbled with pen and ink in the humanities, he laid his finger on the vulnerable spot.

"I was thinking more," he said, "of what you had trusted him to do - telling certain persons, I mean, that you were not dead. He is just as likely as not to have suppressed the information."

Jem Agar was looking very grave, with a sudden pinched appearance about the lips which was only half concealed by his moustache.

"Why should he do that?" he asked sharply.

"He would do it if it suited his purpose. He is not the man to take into consideration such things as feelings - especially the feelings of others."

"You're a bit hard on him, Ruthine," said Jem doubtfully. "Why should it suit his convenience?"

"Secrecy was essential for your purpose and his; in telling a secret one doubles the risk of its disclosure each time a new confidant is admitted. Besides, the man's nature is quite extraordinarily secretive. He has Jewish and Scotch blood in his veins, and the result is that he would rather disseminate false news than true on the off chance of benefiting thereby later on. For men of that breed each piece of accurate information, however trivial, has a marketable value, and they don't part with it unless they get their price."

There followed a silence, during which Jem Agar went back in mental retrospection to the only interview he had ever had with Seymour Michael, and the old lurking sense of distrust awoke within his heart.

"But," said the Captain, who was an optimist - he even applied that theory to human nature - "I suppose it is all right now. Everybody knows now that you are among the quick - eh?"

"No," replied Jem, "only Michael; it was arranged that I should telegraph to him."

"Of course," the Doctor hastened to say, for he had perceived a change in Agar's demeanour, "all this is the purest supposition. It is only a theory built upon a man's character. It is wonderful how consistent people are. Judge how a man would act and you will find that he has acted like it afterwards."

As if in illustration of the theory Jem Agar looked gravely determined, but uttered no threat directed towards Seymour Michael. His quiet face was a threat in itself.

"Well," he said, rising, "I am keeping you fellows from your slumbers. I am still sleeping on deck; can't get accustomed to the atmosphere below decks after six months' sleeping in the open."

He nodded and left them.

"Rum chap!" muttered the Captain, looking at his watch when the footsteps had died away over the silent decks.

"One of the queerest specimens I know," retorted Dr. Mark Ruthine, who was fingering a pen and looking longingly towards the inkstand. The Captain - a man of renowned discretion - quietly departed.

There is no more distrustful man than the simple gentleman of honour who finds himself deceived and tricked. It is as if the bottom suddenly fell out of his trust in all mankind, and there is nothing left but a mocking void. Jem Agar lay on his mattress beneath the awning, and stared hard at a bright star near the horizon. He was realising that life is, after all, a sorry thing of chance, and that all his world might be hanging at that moment on the word of an untrustworthy man.

Before morning he had determined to telegraph from Malta to Seymour Michael to meet him at Plymouth on the arrival of the *Mahanaddy* at that port.

CHAPTER XXVI

BALANCING ACCOUNTS

And yet God has not said a word.

One fine morning in June the *Mahanaddy* steamed with stately deliberation into the calm water inside Plymouth breakwater. Many writers love to dwell with pathetic insistence on incidents of a departure; but there is also pathos - perhaps deeper and truer because more subtle - in the arrival of the homeward-board ship.

Who can tell? There may have been others as anxious to look on the green slopes of Mount Edgecumbe as the man with the mahogany-coloured face who stood ever smoking - smoking - always at the forward starboard corner of the hurricane deck. His story had not leaked out, because only two men on board knew it - men with no conversational leaks whatever. He had made no other friends. But many watched him half interestedly, and perhaps a few divined the great calm impatience beneath the suppressed quiet of his manner.

"That man - Jem Agar - is dangerous," the Doctor had said to the Captain more than once, and Mark Ruthine was not often egregiously mistaken in such matters.

"Um!" replied the Captain of the *Mahanaddy*. "There is an uncanny calm."

They were talking about him now as the Captain - his own pilot for Plymouth and the Channel - walked slowly backwards and forwards on the bridge. It seemed quite natural for the Doctor to be sitting on the rail by the engine-room telegraph. The passengers and the men were quite accustomed to it. This friendship was a matter of history to the homeless world of men and women who travelled east and west through the Suez Canal.

"He has asked me," the Doctor was saying, "to go ashore with him at Plymouth; I don't know why. I imagine he is a little bit afraid of wringing Seymour Michael's neck."

"Just as likely as not," observed the Captain. "It would be a good thing done, but don't let Agar do it."

"May I leave the ship at Plymouth?" asked Mark Ruthine, with a quiet air of obedience which seemed to be accepted with the gravity with which it was offered.

"I don't see why you should not," was the reply. "Everybody goes ashore there except about half a dozen men, who certainly will not want your services."

"I should rather like to do it. We come from the same part of the country, and Agar seems anxious to have me. He is not a chap to say much, but I imagine there will be some sort of a *denouement*."

The Captain was looking through a pair of glasses ahead, towards the anchorage.

Henry Seton Merriman

"All right," he said. "Go."

And he continued to attend to his business with that watchful care which made the *Mahanaddy* one of the safest boats afloat.

Presently Mark Ruthine left the bridge and went to his cabin to pack. As he descended he paused, and retracing his steps forward he went and touched Jem Agar on the arm.

"It's all right," he said. "I'll go with you."

Agar nodded. He was gazing at the green English hills and far faint valley of the Tamar with a curious gleam of excitement in his eyes.

Half an hour later they landed.

"You stick by me," said Jem Agar, when they discerned the small wiry form of Seymour Michael awaiting them on the quay. "I want you to hear everything."

This man was, as Ruthine had said, dangerous. He was too calm. There was something grand and terrifying in that white heat which burned in his eyes and drove the blood from his lips.

Seymour Michael came forward with his pleasant smile, waving his hand in greeting to Jem and to Ruthine, whom he knew.

Jem shook hands with him.

" I'm all right, thanks, " he said curtly, in answer to

Seymour Michael's inquiry.

"Good business - good business," exclaimed the General, who seemed somewhat unnecessarily excited.

"Old Mark Ruthine too!" he went on. "You look as fit as ever. Still turning your thousands out of the British public - eh!"

"Yes," said Ruthine, "thank you."

"Just run ashore for half an hour, I suppose?" continued Seymour Michael, looking hurriedly out towards the *Mahanaddy*.

"No," replied Ruthine, "I leave the ship here."

The small man glanced from the face of one to the other with something sly and uneasy in his eyes.

Jem Agar had altered since he saw him last in the little tent far up on the slopes of the Pamir. He was older and graver. There was also a wisdom in his eyes - that steadfast wise look that comes to eyes which have looked too often on death. Mark Ruthine he knew, and him he distrusted, with that quiet keenness of observation which was his.

"Now," he said eagerly to Jem, "what I thought we might do was to have a little breakfast and catch the eleven o'clock train up to town. If Ruthine will join us, I for one shall be very pleased. He won't mind our talking shop."

Mark Ruthine was attending to the luggage, which was being piled upon a cab.

"Have you not had breakfast?" asked Agar.

"Well, I have had a little, but I don't mind a second edition. That waiter chap at the hotel got me out of bed much too soon. However, it is worth getting up the night before to see you back, old chap."

"Is there not an earlier train than the eleven o'clock?" asked Agar, looking at his watch. There was a singular constraint in his manner which Seymour Michael could not understand.

"Yes, there is one at nine forty-five."

"Then let us go by that. We can get something at the station, if we want it."

"Make it a bottle of champagne to celebrate the return of the explorer, and I am your man," said Michael heartily.

"Make it anything you like," answered Agar, in a gentler voice. He was beginning to come under the influence of Seymour Michael's sweet voice, and of that fascination which nearly all educated Jews unconsciously exercise.

He turned and beckoned to Mark Ruthine, who presently joined them, after paying the boatmen.

"The nine forty-five is the train," he said to him. "We may as well walk up. The streets of Plymouth are not pleasant to drive through."

So the cab was sent on with the luggage, and the three men turned to the slope that leads up to the Hoe.

There was some sort of constraint over them, and they reached the summit of the ascent without having exchanged a word.

When they stood on the Hoe, where the old Eddystone lighthouse is now erected, Seymour Michael turned and looked out over the bay where the ships lay at anchor.

"The good old *Mahanaddy*," he said, "the finest ship I have ever sailed in."

Neither man answered him, but they turned also and looked, standing one on each side of him.

Then at last Jem Agar spoke, breaking a silence which had been brooding since the *Mahanaddy* came out of the Canal.

"I want to know," he said, "exactly how things stand with my people at home."

He continued to look out over the bay towards the *Mahanaddy*, but Mark Ruthine was looking at Seymour Michael.

"Yes," replied the General, "I wanted to talk to you about that. That was really my reason for proposing that we should wait till the second train."

"There cannot be much to say," said Jem Agar rather coldly.

"Well, I wanted to tell you all about it."

"About what?"

There was what the Captain had called an uncanny calm in the voice. General Michael did not answer, and Jem turned slowly towards him.

"I presume," he said, "that I am right in taking it for granted that you have carried out your share of the contract?"

"My dear fellow, it has been perfectly wonderful. The secret has been kept perfectly."

"By all concerned?"

"Eh! - yes."

Michael was glancing furtively at Mark Ruthine, as the fox glances back over his shoulder, not at the huntsman, but at the hounds.

"Did you tell them personally, or did you write?" pursued Jem Agar relentlessly.

"My dear fellow," replied Michael, pulling out his watch, "it is a long story, and we must get to the train."

"No," replied Agar, in the calm voice which raised a sort of "fearful joy" in Ruthine's soul, "we need not be getting to the train yet, and there is no reason for it to be a long story."

Seymour Michael gave an uneasy little laugh, which met with no response whatever. The two taller men exchanged a glance over his head. Up to that moment Jem Agar had hoped for the best. He had a greater faith in human nature than Mark Ruthine had managed to retain.

"Have you or have you not told those people whom you swore to me that you would tell, out there, that night?" asked Jem.

"I told your brother," answered the General with dogged indifference.

"Only?"

There was an ugly gleam in the blue eyes.

"I didn't tell him not to tell the others."

"But you suggested it to him," put in Mark Ruthine, with the knowledge of mankind that was his.

"What has it got to do with you, at any rate?" snapped Seymour Michael.

"Nothing," replied Ruthine, looking across at Agar.

"You did not tell Dora Glynde?"

General Michael shrugged his shoulders.

"Why?" asked Jem hoarsely. It was singular, that sudden hoarseness, and the Doctor, whose business such things were, made a note of it.

"I didn't dare to do it. Why, man, it was too dangerous to tell a single soul. If it had leaked out you would have been murdered up there as sure as hell. There would have been plenty of men ready to do it for half-a-crown."

"That was *my* business," answered Jem coolly. "You

promised, you *swore*, that you would tell Dora Glynde, my step-mother, and my brother Arthur. And you didn't do it. Why?"

"I have given you my reasons - it was too dangerous. Besides, what does it matter? It is all over now."

"No," said Jem, "not yet."

The clock struck nine at that moment; and from the harbour came the sound of the ship's bells, high and clear, sounding the hour. The Hoe was quite deserted; these three men were alone. A silence followed the ringing of the bells, like the silence that precedes a verdict.

Then Jem Agar spoke.

"I asked Mark Buthine," he said, "to come ashore with me, because I had reason to suspect your good faith. I can't see now why you should have done this, but I suppose that people who are born liars, as Ruthine says you are, prefer lying to telling the truth. You are coming down now with Ruthine and myself to Stagholme. I shall tell the whole story as it happened, and then you will have to explain matters to the two ladies as best you can."

A sudden unreasoning terror took possession of Seymour Michael. He knew that one of the ladies was Anna Agar, the woman who hated him almost as much as he deserved. He was afraid of her; for it is one consolation to the wronged to know that the wronger goes all through his life with a dull, unquenchable fear upon his heart. But this was not sufficient, this could not account for the mighty terror which clutched his soul at that moment, and he knew it. He felt that this was something beyond that - something which could not be reasoned away. It was a physical terror, one of those emotions which seem to attack the body independently of the soul, a terror striking the Man before it reaches the Mind. His limbs trembled; it was only by an effort that he kept his teeth clenched to prevent them from chattering.

"And," said Jem Agar, "if I find that any harm has been done - if any one has suffered for this, I will give you the soundest thrashing you have ever had in your life."

Both his hearers knew now who Dora Glynde was, what she was to him. He neither added to their knowledge nor sought to mislead. He was not, as we have said, *de ceux qui s'expliquent*.

"Come," he added, and turning he led the way across the Hoe.

Seymour Michael followed quietly. He was cowed by the inward fear which would not be allayed, and the judicial calmness of these two men paralysed him. Once, in the train, he began explaining matters over again.

"We will hear all that at Stagholme," said Jem sternly, and Mark Ruthine merely looked at him over the top of a newspaper which he was not reading.

CHAPTER XXVII

AT BAY

To thine own self be true;
And it must follow as the night the day
Thou canst not then be false to any man.

Human nature is, after all, a hopeless failure. Not even
the very best instinct is safe. It will probably be turned
sooner or later to evil account.

The best instinct in Anna Agar was her maternal love,
and upon this strong rock she finally wrecked her
barque. She was one of those women who hold that, so
long as the object is unselfish, the means used to obtain
it cannot well be evil. She did not say this in so many
words, because she was quite without principle, good
or bad, and she invariably acted on impulse.

Her impulse at this time was to turn as much of heaven
and earth as came under her influence to compel Dora
to marry Arthur. That Arthur should be unhappy, and
should be allowed to continue in that common
condition, was a thought that she could not tolerate or
allow. Something must be done, and it was
characteristic of the woman that that something should
present itself to her in the form of the handy and useful
lie. In a strait we all naturally turn to that

accomplishment in which we consider ourselves most proficient. The blusterer blusters; the profane man swears; the tearful woman weeps - and weeping, by the way, is no mean accomplishment if it be used at the right moment. Mrs. Agar naturally meditated on that form of diplomacy which is sometimes called lying. The truth would not serve her purpose (not that she had given it a fair trial), and therefore she would forsake the straight path for that other one which hath many turnings.

Dora absolutely refused to come to Stagholme while Arthur was there - a delicacy of feeling, which, by the way, was quite incomprehensible to Mrs. Agar. It was necessary for Arthur's happiness that he should see Dora again and try the effect of another necktie and further eloquence. Therefore, Dora must be made by subterfuge to see Arthur.

"Dear Dora," she wrote, "it will be a great grief to me if this unfortunate attachment of my poor boy's is allowed to interfere with the affection which has existed between us since your infancy. Come, dear, and see me to-morrow afternoon. I shall be quite alone, and the subject which, of course, occupies the first place in my thoughts will, if you wish it, be tabooed.

"Your affectionate old Friend,

"ANNA AGAR."

"It will be quite easy," reflected this diplomatic lady as she folded the letter - almost illegible on account of its impetuosity - "for Arthur to come back from East Burgen earlier than I expected him."

The rest she left to chance, which was very kind but not quite necessary, for chance had already taken possession of the rest, and was even at that moment making her arrangements.

Dora read the letter in the garden beneath the laburnum-tree, where she spent a large part of her life. Before reaching the end of the epistle she had determined to go. She was a young person of spirit as well as of discrimination, and in obedience to the urging of the former was quite ready to show Mrs. Agar, and Arthur too, if need be, that she was not afraid of them.

She was distinctly conscious of the increasing power of her own strength of purpose as she made this resolution, and as she walked across the park the next afternoon her feeling was one very near akin to elation. It is only the strong who mistrust their own power. Dora Glynde had always looked upon herself as a somewhat weak and easily led person; she was beginning to feel her own strength now and to rejoice in it. From the first she half-suspected a trap of some sort. Such a subterfuge was eminently characteristic of Mrs. Agar, and that lady's manner of welcoming her only increased the suspicion.

The mistress of Stagholme was positively crackling with an excitement which even her best friend could not have called suppressed. There was no suppression whatever about it.

"So good of you," she panted, "to come, Dora dear!"

And she searched madly for her pocket handkerchief.

"Not at all," replied Dora, very calmly.

"And now, dear," went on the lady of the house, "are we going to talk about it?"

The question was somewhat futile, for it was easy to see that she was not in a condition to talk of anything else.

"I think not," replied Dora. She had a way of using the word "think" when she was positive. "The question was raised the last time I saw you, and I do not think that any good resulted from it."

Mrs. Agar's face dropped. In some ways she was a child still, and a childish woman of fifty is as aggravating a creature as walks upon this earth. Dora remembered every word of the interview referred to, while Mrs. Agar had almost forgotten it. It is to the common-minded that common proverbs and sayings of the people apply. Hard words had not the power of breaking anything in Mrs. Agar's being.

"Of course," she said, "*I* don't wish to talk about it, if you don't. It is most painful to me."

She had dragged forward a second chair, only separated from that occupied by Dora by the tea-table.

"Arthur," she said, with a lamentable assumption of cheerfulness, "has driven over to East Burgen to get some things I wanted. He will not be back for ever so long."

She reflected that he was overdue at that moment, and that the butler had orders to send him to the library as soon as he returned.

"I was sorry to hear," said Dora, quite naturally, "that he had not passed his examination."

Mrs. Agar glanced at her cunningly; she was always looking for second meanings in the most innocent remarks, hardly guilty of an original meaning.

At this moment the door leading through a smaller library into the dining-room opened and Arthur came quietly in. He changed colour and hesitated, but only for a moment. Then he remembered that before all things a gentleman must be a gentleman. He came forward and held out his hand.

"How do you do?" he said, and for a moment he was quite dignified. "I am glad to see you here with mother. I did not know that I was going to interrupt a *téte-à-téte*, tea. No tea, thanks, mother; no."

"Have you brought the things I wanted? You are earlier than I expected," blurted out the lady of the house unskillfully.

"Yes, I have brought them."

"I must go and see if they are right," said Mrs. Agar, rising, and before he could stop her she passed out of the door by which he had entered.

For a moment there was an awkward silence, then Dora spoke - after the door had been reluctantly closed from without.

"I suppose," she said, "that this was done on purpose?"

"Not by me, Dora."

She merely bowed her head.

"Do you believe me?" he asked.

"Yes."

She continued to sip her tea, and he actually handed her a plate of biscuits.

"Is it still No?" he asked abruptly.

"Yes."

Perhaps her fresh youthful beauty moved him, perhaps it was merely opposition that raised his love suddenly to the dignity of a passion that made him for once forget himself, his clothes, his personal appearance, and the gentlemanly modulation of his voice.

For a moment he was almost a man. He almost touched the height of a man's ascendency over woman.

"You may say No now," he cried, "but I shall have you yet. Some day you will say Yes."

It was then for the first time that Dora realised that this man did actually love her according to his lights. But never for an instant did she admit in her own mind the possibility of succumbing to Arthur's will. It is not by words that men command women. They must first command their respect, and that is never gained by words.

Dora was conscious of a feeling of sudden,

Henry Seton Merriman

unspeakable pain. Arthur had only succeeded in convincing her that she could have submitted to a man's will, wholly and without reserve; but not to the will of Arthur Agar. He had only showed her that such a submission would in itself have been a greater happiness than she had ever tasted. But she knew at once that only one man ever had, ever could have had, the power of exacting such submission; and he commanded it, not by word of mouth (for he never seemed to ask it), but by something strong and just and good within himself, before which her whole being bowed down.

We never know how we appear in the eyes of our neighbours, friends or lovers. Arthur was at that moment in Dora's eyes a mere sham, aping something he could never attain.

He had seized her two hands in his nervous and delicate fingers, from which she easily withdrew them. The action was natural enough, strong enough. But he completely spoiled the effect by the words he spoke in his thin tenor voice.

"No, Arthur," she said. "No, Arthur; since you mention the future, I may as well tell you *now* that my answer will never be anything but No. At one time I thought that it might be different. I told my mother that possibly, after a great many years, I might think otherwise; but I retract that. I shall never think otherwise. And if you imagine that you can force me to do so, please lay aside that hope at once."

"Then there is some one else!" cried Arthur, with an apparent irrelevance. "I know there is some one else."

Dora seemed to be reflecting. She looked over his head, out of the window, where the fleecy summer clouds floated idly over the sky.

She turned and looked deliberately at the door by which Mrs. Agar had disappeared. It was standing ajar. Then again she reflected, weighing something in her mind.

"Yes," she replied half-dreamily at length. "I think you have a right to know - there is some one else."

"Was," corrected Arthur, with the womanly intuition which was given to him with other womanly traits.

"Was and is," replied Dora quietly. "His being dead makes no difference so far as you are concerned."

"Then it *was* Jem! I was sure it was Jem," said a third voice.

In the excitement of the moment Mrs. Agar forgot that when ladies and gentlemen stoop to eavesdropping they generally retire discreetly and return after a few moments, humming a tune, hymns preferred.

"I knew that you were there," said Dora, with a calmness which was not pleasant to the ear. "I saw your black dress through the crack of the door. You did not stand quite still, which was a pity, because the sunlight was on the floor behind you. I was not surprised; it was worthy of you."

"I take God to witness," cried Mrs. Agar, "that I only heard the last words as I came back into the room."

"Don't," said Dora, "that is blasphemy."

"Arthur," cried Mrs. Agar, "will you hear your mother called names?"

"We will not wrangle," said Dora, rising with something very like a smile on her face. "Yes, if you want to know, it *was* Jem. I have only his memory, but still I can be faithful to that. I don't care if all the world knows; that is why I told *you* behind the door. I am not ashamed of it. I always did care for Jem."

There was a little pause, for mother and son had nothing to answer. Dora turned to take her gloves, which she had laid on a side table, and as she did so the other door opened, the principal door leading to the hall. Moreover, it was opened without the menial pause, and they all turned in surprise, knowing that there were only servants in the house.

In the doorway stood Jem, brown-faced, lean, and anxious-looking. There was something wolf-like in his face, with the fierce blue eyes shining from beneath dark lashes, the fair moustache pushed forward by set lips.

Behind him the keen face of Seymour Michael peered nervously, restlessly from side to side. He was distinctly suggestive of a rat in a trap. And beyond him, in the gloom of the old arras-hung hall, a third man, seemingly standing guard over Seymour Michael, for he was not looking into the room but watching every movement made by the General - tall man, dark, upright, with a silent, clean-shaven face, a total stranger to them all. But his manner was not that of a stranger, he seemed to have something to do there.

CHAPTER XXVIII

THE LAST LINK

A thing hereditary in the race comes unawares.

Jem came straight into the room, and there seemed to be no one in it for him but Dora. She went to meet him with outstretched hand, and her eyes were answering the questions that she read in his.

He took her hand and he said no word, but suddenly all the misery of the last year slipped back, as it were, into a dream. She could not define her thoughts then, and they left no memory to recall afterwards. She seemed to forget that this man had been dead and was living, she only knew that her hand was within his. Jem looked round to the others present, his attitude a judgment in itself, his face, in its fierce repose, a verdict.

Mark Ruthine had gently pushed Seymour Michael into the room and was closing the door behind them. Mrs. Agar did not see the General, who was half-concealed by his junior officer. She could not take her eyes from Jem's face.

"This is fortunate," he said; and the sound of his voice was music in Dora's ears. "This is fortunate, every one

Henry Seton Merriman

seems to be here."

He paused for a moment, as if at a loss, and drew his brown hand down over his moustache. Perhaps he felt remotely that his position was strong and almost dramatic; but that, being a simple, honest Englishman, he was unable to turn it to account.

He turned towards Seymour Michael, who stood behind, uncomfortably conscious of Mark Ruthine at his heels. It was not in Jem to make an effective scene. Englishmen are so. We do not make our lives superficially picturesque by apostrophising the shade of a dead mother. Jem gave way to the natural instinct of a soldier by nature and training. A clear statement of the facts, and a short, sharp judgment.

"This man," he said, laying his hand on the General's shoulder, and bringing him forward, "has been brought here by us to explain something."

White-lipped, breathless, in a ghastly silence Anna Agar and Seymour Michael stared at each other over the dainty tea-table, across a gulf of misused years, through the tangle of two unfaithful lives.

Then Jem Agar began his story, addressing himself to Dora, then, and until the end.

"I was not with Stevenor," he said, "when his force was surprised and annihilated. I had been sent on through an enemy's country into a position which no man had the right to ask another to hold with the force allowed me. This man sent me. All his life has he been seeking glory at the risk of other men's lives. After the disaster he came to me and relieved my little force; but he proposed to me a scheme of exploration, which I have carried through. But even now I shall not get the credit; *he* will have that. It was a low, scurrilous thing to do; for he was my commanding officer, and I could not say No."

"I gave you the option," blurted out Michael sullenly.

Jem took no notice of the interruption, which only had the effect of making Mark Ruthine move up a few paces nearer.

"He made a great point of secrecy," continued Agar, "which at the time I thought to be for my safety. But now I see otherwise; Ruthine has pointed it out to me. If I had never come back he would have said nothing, and would thus have escaped the odium of having sent a man to certain death. I only made one condition - namely, that three persons should be informed at once of my survival, after the disaster to Stevenor's force. Those three persons were my brother Arthur, my stepmother, and Miss Glynde."

He paused for a moment, and Dora's clear, low voice took up the narrative.

"I met General Michael," she said, "in London, some months ago. I met him more than once. He knew quite well who I was, and he never told me."

Thus was the first link of the chain riveted. Seymour Michael winced. He never raised his eyes.

Mark Ruthine moved forward again. He did so with a singular rapidity, for he had seen murder flash from beneath Jem Agar's eyebrows. He was standing between them, his left hand gripping Jem's right arm with an undeniable strength. Dora, looking at them, suddenly felt the tears well to her eyes. There was something that melted her heart strangely in the sight of those two men - friends - standing side by side; and at that moment her affection went out towards Mark Ruthine, the friend of Jem, who understood Jem, who knew Jem and loved him, perhaps, a thousandth part as well as she did; an affection which was never withdrawn all through their lives.

It was Ruthine's voice that broke the silence, giving Jem time to master himself.

"It is to his credit," he said, also addressing Dora, "that for very shame he did not dare to tell you that he had sent Agar on a mission which was as unnecessary as it was dangerous. When he sent him he must have known that it was almost a sentence of death."

Then Jem spoke again.

"As soon as I got back to civilisation," he said, "I wrote to him as arranged, and I enclosed letters to - the three persons who were admitted into the secret. Those letters have, of course, never reached their destination. General Michael will be required to explain that also."

At this moment Arthur Agar gave a strange little cackling laugh, which drew the general attention towards him. He was looking at his half-brother, with a glitter in his usually soft and peaceful eyes.

"There are a good many things which he will have to explain."

"Yes," answered Jem. "That is why we have brought him here."

It fell to Arthur Agar's lot to forge the second link.

"When," he asked Jem, "did he know that you had got back to safety and civilisation?"

"Two months ago, by telegram."

The half-brothers turned with one accord towards Seymour Michael, who stood trying to conceal the quiver of his lips.

"He promised," said Arthur Agar, "to tell me at once when he received news of your safety."

It was singular that Seymour Michael should give way at that moment to a little shrinking movement of fear - back and away, not from Jem, who towered huge and powerful above him, but from the frail and delicate younger brother. Mark Ruthine, who was standing behind, saw the movement and wondered at it. For it would appear that, of all his judges, Seymour Michael feared the weakest most.

And so the second link was welded on to the first, while only Anna Agar knew the motive that had prompted Michael to suppress the news. She divined that it was spite towards herself, and for once in her life, with that intuition which only comes at supreme moments, she had the wisdom to bide her time.

Then at last Seymour Michael spoke. He did not raise his eyes, but his words were evidently addressed to Arthur.

"I acted," he said, "as I thought best. Secrecy was necessary for Agar's safety. I knew that if I told you too much you would tell your mother, and - I know your mother better than either you or Jem Agar know her. She is not fit to be trusted with the most trifling secret."

"Well, you see, you were quite wrong," burst out Mrs. Agar, with a derisive laugh. "For I knew it all along. Arthur told me at the first."

Her voice came as a shock to them all. It was harsh and common, the voice of the street-wrangler.

"Then," cried Seymour Michael, as sharp as fate, "why did you not tell Miss Glynde?"

He raised his arm, pointing one lean dark finger into her face.

"I knew," he hissed, "that the boy would tell you. I counted on it. Why did you not tell Miss Glynde? Come! Tell us why."

Mark Ruthine's face was a study. It was the face of a very keen sportsman at the corner of a "drive." In every word he saw twice as much as simple Jem Agar ever suspected.

"Well," answered Mrs. Agar, wavering, "because I thought it better not."

"No," Dora said, "you kept it from me because you wanted me to marry Arthur. And you thought that I should do so because he was master of Stagholme. You wanted to trick me into marrying Arthur before" - she hesitated - "before -"

"Before I came back," added Jem imperturbably. "That was it, that was it!" cried Seymour Michael, grasping at the straw which might serve to turn the current aside from himself.

But the attempt failed. No one took any notice of it. Jem was looking at Dora, and she was looking anywhere except at him.

It was Jem who spoke, with the decisiveness of the president of a court-martial.

"That will come afterwards," he said. "And now, perhaps," he went on, turning towards Seymour, "you will kindly explain why you broke your word to me. Explain it to these l - [sic.] to Miss Glynde."

Seymour Michael shrugged his shoulders.

"Why, what is the good of making all this fuss about it now?" he explained. "It has all come right. I acted as I thought best. That is all the explanation I have to offer."

"Can you not do better than that?" inquired Jem, with a dangerous suavity. "You had better try."

Dora was looking at Jem now, appealingly. She knew that tone of voice, and feared it. She alone suspected the anger that was hidden behind so calm an exterior.

Seymour Michael preserved a dogged silence, glancing from side to side beneath his lowered lashes. He had not forgotten Jem's threat, but he felt the safeguard of a lady's presence.

"I can offer an explanation," put in Mark Ruthine. "This man is mentally incapable of telling the truth and of doing the straight thing. There are some people who are born liars. This man is one. It is not quite fair to judge him as one would judge others. I have known him for years, have watched him, have studied him."

All eyes turned towards Seymour Michael, who stood half-cringing, trembling with fear and hatred towards his relentless judges.

"Years ago," pursued Ruthine, "at the outset of life, he committed a wanton crime. He did a wrong to a poor innocent woman, whose only fault was to love him beyond his deserts. He was engaged to be married to her, and meeting a richer woman he had not the courage to ask to be released from his engagement. It happened that by a mistake he was gazetted 'dead' at the time of the Mutiny. He never contradicted the mistake - that was how he got out of his engagement. He played the same trick with Jem Agar's name. I recognised it."

Then the last link of the chain was forged.

"So did I," said Anna Agar. "I was the woman."

Before the words were well out of her mouth Mark Ruthine's voice was raised in an alarmed shout.

"Look out!" he cried. "Hold that man; he is mad!"

No one had been noticing Arthur Agar - no one except Seymour Michael, who had never taken his eyes from his face during Ruthine's narration.

With a groan, unlike a human sound at all, Arthur Agar had rushed forward when his mother spoke, and for a few seconds there was a wild confusion in the room, while Seymour Michael, white with dread, fled before his doom. In and out among the people and the furniture, shouting for help, he leapt and struggled. Then there came a crash. Seymour Michael had broken through the window, smashing the glass, with his arms doubled over his face.

A second later Arthur wrenched open the sash and gave chase across the lawn. In the confusion some moments elapsed before the two heavier men followed him over the smooth turf, and the ladies from the window saw Arthur Agar kneeling over Seymour Michael on the stone terrace at the end of the lawn. They heard with cruel distinctness the sharp crackling crash of the Jew's head upon the stone flags, as Arthur shook him as a terrier shakes a rat.

Instinctively they followed, and as they came up to the group where Ruthine was kneeling over Seymour Michael, while Jem dragged Arthur away, they heard the Doctor say -

"Agar, get the ladies away. This man is dead. Look sharp, man! They mustn't see this."

And Jem barred their way with one hand, while he held his half-brother with the other.

CHAPTER XXIX

SETTLED

For love in sequel works with fate.

The four walked back to the library together. Mrs. Agar looked back over her shoulder at every other footstep. She took no notice of her son. Her affection for him seemed suddenly to have been absorbed and lost in some other emotion.

Jem was half supporting, half carrying Arthur, whose eyes were like those of a dead man, while his lips were parted in a vacant, senseless way.

Already Ruthine could be heard giving his orders to the gardeners and other servants who had gathered round him in a wonderfully short space of time.

Dora passed into the library first, treading carefully over the broken glass, and Mrs. Agar followed her without appearing to notice the sound of breakage beneath her feet. No one had spoken a word since Mark Ruthine had told them that Seymour Michael was dead. There are some situations in life wherein we suddenly realise what an inadequate thing human speech is. There are some things that others know which we have never told them, and would ever be unable to tell them. There are some feelings within us for which no language can find expression.

Mrs. Agar was simply stupefied. When God does mete out punishment here on earth, He does so with an overflowing measure. This devoted mother did not even evince anxiety as to the welfare of her son, for whose sake she had made so many blunders, so many futile plots.

Jem brought Arthur into the room, and led him to an arm-chair. There was that steady masterfulness in his manner which comes to those who have looked on death in many forms and whom nothing can dismay.

He offered no unnecessary assistance or advice, did not fussily loosen Arthur's necktie, or perform any of those small inappropriate offices which some would have deemed necessary under the circumstances. He knew quite well that this was no matter of a necktie or a collar.

Mrs. Agar seated herself on a sofa opposite, and slowly swayed her body backwards and forwards. She was one of those persons who can never separate mental anguish from physical pain. They have but one way of expressing both, and possibly of feeling both. Her hands were clasped on her lap, her head on one side, her lips drawn back as if in agony. She even went so far as to breathe laboriously.

Thus they remained; Jem watching Arthur, Dora watching Jem, who seemed to ignore her presence.

It was Mrs. Agar who spoke first, angrily and bitterly.

"What is the good of standing there?" she said to Jem. "Can't you find something more useful to do than that?"

Jem looked at her, first with surprise and then with something very nearly approaching contempt.

"I am waiting," he replied, "for Ruthine. He is a doctor."

"Who wants a doctor now? What is the good of a doctor now - now that Seymour is dead? I don't know what he is doing here, at any rate, meddling."

"Arthur wants a doctor," replied Jem. "Can you not see that he is in a sort of trance? He hears and sees nothing. He is quite unconscious."

Mrs. Agar seemed only half to understand. She stared at her son, swaying backwards and forwards in imbecile misery.

"Oh dear! oh dear!" she whispered, "what have we done to deserve this?"

After a few seconds she repeated the words.

"What have we done to deserve this? What have we done ..."

Her voice died away into a whisper, and when that became inaudible her lips went on moving, still framing the same words over and over again.

In this manner they waited, with that dull senselessness to the flight of time which follows on a great shock.

They all heard the clatter of horses' feet on the gravel of the avenue, and probably they all divined that Mark Ruthine had sent for medical help.

To Dora the sound brought a sudden boundless sense of relief. Amidst this mental confusion it came as a practical common-sense proof that the tension of the last year was over. The burden of her own life was by it lifted from her shoulders; for Jem was here, and nothing could matter very much now.

Presently Ruthine came into the room. As he went towards Arthur he glanced at Dora and then at Mrs. Agar, but the young fellow was evidently his first care.

While he was kneeling by the low chair examining Arthur's eyes and face, Mrs. Agar suddenly rose and crossed the room.

"Is he dead?" she said abruptly.

"Who?" inquired Mark Ruthine, without looking round.

"Seymour Michael."

"Yes."

"Quite?"

"Yes."

"Then Arthur killed him?"

"Yes."

All this while Arthur was lying back in the chair, white and lifeless. His eyes were open, he breathed regularly, but he heard nothing that was said, nor saw anything before his eyes.

"Then," said Mrs. Agar, "that was a murder?"

She was looking out of the window, towards the stone terrace, already conscious that the scene that she had witnessed there would never be effaced from her memory while she had life.

After a little pause Mark Ruthine spoke.

"No," he answered, "it was not that. Your son was not responsible for his actions when he did it. I think I can prove that. I do not yet know what it was. It was very singular. I think it was some sort of mental aberration - temporary, I hope, and think. We will see when he recovers himself - when the circulation is restored."

While he spoke he continued to examine his patient. He spoke in his natural tone, without attempting to lower his voice, for he knew that Arthur Agar had no comprehension of things terrestrial at that time.

"It was not," he went on, "the action of a sane man. Besides, he could not have done it. In his right mind he could not have killed Seymour Michael, who was a strong man. As it is, I think that there was some sort of paralysis in Seymour Michael - a paralysis of fear. He seemed too frightened to attempt to defend himself. Besides, why should your son do it?"

"He was born hating him."

Mark Ruthine slowly turned, still upon his knees. He rose, and in his dark face there was that strange eagerness again, like the eagerness of a sportsman approaching some unknown quarry in the jungle.

"What do you mean, Mrs. Agar?" he asked.

"I mean that he was born with a hatred for that man stronger than anything that was in him. His soul was given to him full of hate for Seymour Michael. Such things are when a woman bears a child in the midst of great passion."

"Yes," said Mark Ruthine, "I know."

"The night he was born," Mrs. Agar went on, "I first saw and spoke to that man after he had come back from India - after I had learnt what he had done."

Ruthine turned round towards Jem and Dora.

"You hear that," he said to them. "This is not the story of a mother trumped up in court to save her son. It is the truth. There are some things which we do not understand even yet. Don't forget what you have heard. It will come in usefully."

He turned to Mrs. Agar again.

"Did he know the story?" he asked.

"He never heard it until you told it just now."

"Can you swear to that, Mrs. Agar?"

"Yes."

"Then," said Ruthine, "he does not know now that you are the woman whom Seymour Michael wronged. He need never know it. The paroxysm had come on before you spoke - that was why I shouted. He was mad with hate, before you opened your lips."

Mrs. Agar was now beginning to realise what was at stake. The mother's love was re-awakening. The old cunning look came into her eyes, and her quick, truthless mind was evidently on the alert. There was something animal-like in Mrs. Agar; but she was of the lower order of animal, that seeks to defend its young by cunning and not by sheer bravery.

Ruthine must have guessed at something, for he said at once:

"Remember what you have told me. You will have to repeat that exactly. Add nothing to it, take nothing from it, or you will spoil it. Tell me, has your son seen this man more than once?"

"No, only once; at Cambridge."

"All right; I think I shall be able to prove it."

As he spoke he went towards the writing-table and, sitting down, he wrote out a prescription. Dora followed him and held out her hand for the paper.

"Send for that at once, please," he said.

Then he beckoned to Jem.

"I have sent for the local doctor," he said to him. "But I should advise having some one else - Llandoller from

Harley Street. This is far above our heads."

"Telegraph for him," answered Jem Agar.

While Ruthine wrote he went on speaking.

"We must get him upstairs at once," he said. "I should like to have him in bed before the doctor comes."

In answer to the bell, rung a second time, the servant came, looking white and scared.

"Show Dr. Ruthine Mr. Arthur's room," said Jem; and Ruthine took Arthur up in his arms like a child.

When they had gone there was a silence. Mrs. Agar made no attempt to follow. She sat down again on the sofa, swaying backwards and forwards. Perhaps she was dimly aware that there remained something still to be said.

Jem Agar crossed the room and stood in front of her. Dora, from the background, was pleading with her eyes for this woman. There were the makings of a very hard man in James Edward Makerstone Agar, and seven years of the grimmest soldiering of modern days had done nothing to soften him. He was strictly just; but it is not justice that women want. To all men there comes a time when they recognise the fact that all their time and all their energies are required for the taking care of *one* woman, and that all the rest must take care of themselves.

"You may stay," he said to his step-mother, "until Arthur is removed from this house - but no longer. I shall never pretend to forgive you, and I never want to see you again."

Mrs. Agar made no answer, nor did she look up.

"Go," said Jem, with a little jerk of his head towards the door.

Slowly she rose, and without looking at either of them she passed out of the room.

When, at last, they were left alone in the quiet library where they had played together as children, where the happiest moments of his life and the most miserable of hers had been lived through.

Dora did not seem to know quite what to do. She was standing by the writing-table, with one hand resting on it, facing him, but not looking at him. She suddenly felt unable to do that - felt at a loss, abashed, unequal to the moment.

But Jem seemed to have no hesitation. He was quite natural and very deliberate. He seemed to know quite well what to do. He closed the door behind Mrs. Agar, and then he came across the room and took Dora in his arms, as if there were no question about it. He said nothing. After all, there was nothing to be said.

www.ingramcontent.com/pod-product-compliance
Lightning Source LLC
Chambersburg PA
CBHW030114180626
46812CB00002B/408